BOOKS BY BELINDA MURRELL

Pippa's Island

Book 1: The Beach Shack Cafe
Book 2: Cub Reporters
Book 3: Kira Dreaming

The Locket of Dreams
The Ruby Talisman
The Ivory Rose
The Forgotten Pearl
The River Charm
The Sequin Star
The Lost Sapphire

The Sun Sword Trilogy

Book 1: The Quest for the Sun Gem
Book 2: The Voyage of the Owl
Book 3: The Snowy Tower

Lulu Bell

Lulu Bell and the Birthday Unicorn
Lulu Bell and the Fairy Penguin
Lulu Bell and the Cubby Fort
Lulu Bell and the Moon Dragon
Lulu Bell and the Circus Pup
Lulu Bell and the Sea Turtle
Lulu Bell and the Tiger Cub
Lulu Bell and the Pyjama Party
Lulu Bell and the Christmas Elf
Lulu Bell and the Koala Joey
Lulu Bell and the Arabian Nights
Lulu Bell and the Magical Garden
Lulu Bell and the Pirate Fun

BOOK 3

PIPPA'S ISLAND

KIRA DREAMING

BELINDA MURRELL

RANDOM HOUSE AUSTRALIA

A Random House book
Published by Penguin Random House Australia Pty Ltd
Level 3, 100 Pacific Highway, North Sydney NSW 2060
www.penguin.com.au

Penguin
Random House
Australia

First published by Random House Australia in 2018

Addresses for the Penguin Random House group of companies can be found at
global.penguinrandomhouse.com/offices.

National Library of Australia
Cataloguing-in-Publication entry

Creator: Murrell, Belinda, author
Title: Kira dreaming / Belinda Murrell
ISBN: 978 0 14378 370 1 (pbk)
Series: Murrell, Belinda. Pippa's Island; 3
Target audience: For primary school age
Subjects: Friendship – Juvenile fiction
            Coffee shops – Juvenile fiction
            Island life – Juvenile fiction

Cover and internal design by Christabella Designs
Cover and internal images: two girls in ballet dresses Focus and Blur/Shutterstock;
young brunette girl with watermelon Andrey Arkusha/Shutterstock; young
magician performing a trick Nagy-Bagoly Arpad/Shutterstock; microphone and
female singer Golubovy/Shutterstock; journal cards Ksenia Lokko/Shutterstock;
summer cards Ksenia Lokko/Shutterstock; hand-drawn summer creative
alphabet Ksenia Lokko/Shutterstock
Typeset by Midland Typesetters, Australia
Printed in Australia by Griffin Press, an accredited ISO AS/NZS 14001:2004
Environmental Management System printer

Penguin Random House Australia uses papers that are natural, renewable
and recyclable products and made from wood grown in sustainable forests.
The logging and manufacturing processes are expected to conform to the
environmental regulations of the country of origin.

For the best brother ever – Nick Humphrey.
A big thank you for all your love,
inspiration, and support.

Have you ever wanted to start a club? One with the very best friends anyone could wish for? It's the most brilliant fun!

My three best friends are Charlie, Meg and Cici and we are all in year five at Kira Cove Primary School. A few weeks ago, we started our own secret club. We call ourselves the Sassy Sisters and our motto is 'Be bold! Be brave! And be full of happy spirit!' The four of us meet after school every Friday to talk and laugh, share our problems and eat lots of yummy food. (Cici is the best cupcake baker ever!)

Since we became the Sassy Sisters we've had loads of adventures together - helping my mum to start the Beach Shack Cafe, kayaking, surfing and hanging out at the beach, doing challenging projects at school and writing stories for the school newspaper. We even performed with our favourite pop singer, Ruby Starr, which was terrifying and exciting and amazing all at once.

Having a group of best friends is fantastic. But it can be tricky sometimes, especially when they want to do something that you definitely don't want to do! That was the trouble I found myself in when Cici (our star performer) had one of her mad ideas. Charlie loves to sing and play the guitar, too, so of course she and Cici were super-excited when it was announced that Kira Cove Primary School would be holding a talent quest. Meg is the peacemaker in our gang and she just wants everyone to get along. Whereas me? Well, I wasn't quite so keen on the idea.

Despite our differences, the Sassy Sisters have made life on Kira Island so much fun. My mum, Harry, Bella and I only moved here a few months ago and it hasn't been easy. For the moment, we are still living in a caravan in the back garden of my grandparents' cottage while our new home is being renovated. The four of us are crammed into a tiny space, together with our wild and wicked puppy, Summer. It sounds like crazy chaos - and it is! Life is never boring in the Hamilton family.

Pippa

CHAPTER 1

CICI'S BRILLIANT IDEA

It was Friday afternoon. My favourite time of the week. The four of us joked and laughed as we walked home from school to Charlie's house for our weekly Sassy Sisters club meeting. We took it in turns to meet at our different homes. On Meg's yacht, bobbing in the harbour. In Cici's sweet-smelling kitchen. And, of course, at the Beach Shack Cafe with our favourite mango smoothies and cupcakes for afternoon tea.

Charlie lived in a sprawling house on top of the island's plateau, surrounded by gardens and paddocks. The house had to be big because there were five kids in her family. Charlie has a sister, Sophia, two step-brothers, Sebastian and Oscar, and a half-sister called Daisy. Seb is in year six, Sophia and Oscar are both in year four, and Daisy is in year one. Charlie's family also has a menagerie of pets – two donkeys, two dogs, five chickens, a cat called Trixie and a lamb called Maisie. Charlie warned us about how noisy her place could get. She wasn't wrong.

Cici, Meg and I were sitting around the kitchen table. Trixie, the calico cat, was rubbing her head against my leg. I leaned down and picked her up for a cuddle. She purred and rubbed her cheek against my chin. Trixie is the prettiest cat with her fur coloured in patches of white, black and ginger.

Charlie was looking in the fridge for some snacks for afternoon tea.

'Mum?' called Charlie. 'Do you know where the hummus is?'

'In the fridge,' called back her mum, Jodie, from the office where she was working. 'Top shelf.'

Jodie is a graphic designer and helped my mum design all the menus and signage for the cafe.

'It's not there,' said Charlie, rummaging through the containers on the top shelf.

'I bought it this morning,' said Jodie, sticking her head around the corner. 'It should be there on the right-hand side.'

Charlie shook her head. 'I can't find it.'

'Let me have a look,' said Jodie. But the hummus had disappeared.

Sophia, Seb and Oscar raced through the kitchen, followed closely by Zorro and Bandit, the two border collies. Trixie turned her back on the rowdy interlopers, ignoring them completely. She batted my hand with her paw, begging for another snuggle.

'Kids, did any of you eat the hummus?' asked Jodie. Sophia looked guiltily at Seb.

Seb tried to look innocent. 'Hummus? What hummus?'

Oscar gave a cheeky grin. He clearly knew something about the missing snack. 'I'd love some, thanks, Jodie. I'm starving.'

Jodie went back to searching through the fridge. 'I know it's here somewhere.'

Charlie looked at the boys suspiciously. Seb rubbed his tummy.

'Seb, Mum bought the hummus especially because the girls were coming over,' said Charlie. 'I bet you guys scoffed the lot.'

'Would we do that?' asked Seb, pretending to be hurt by the accusation.

'*Yes*,' said Charlie, tossing her long blonde plait over her shoulder.

The hummus, of course, was nowhere to be found, so Jodie cut up some strawberries and pineapple for us. Then she went back to work in her study. Charlie's three siblings raced past once more, Seb snatching a handful of pine-apple on the way through.

'Back to our meeting,' said Charlie with a sniff of disapproval. I picked up my pen to take notes. It was my job as Keeper of the Sassy Sister Notebook to jot down our ideas and plans, although today I spent more time doodling in the margins while we chatted.

Charlie was the current President of the Sassy Sisters. Meg was Vice President and Research Officer, and Cici was Treasurer (not that we had any money) and Chief Cupcake Baker.

Just then Charlie's little sister, Daisy, came in and plonked herself down at the table. Daisy was great friends with my sister, Bella.

'Can I have some strawberries, Charlie?' she asked. Charlie rolled her eyes but she jumped up and filled a bowl of fruit for Daisy.

'Here you go, Daisy,' said Charlie with great patience. 'But why don't you go and eat them with Sophia. We're busy now.'

'I don't want to eat them with Sophia. I want to stay here with you and Cici . . . and Pippa and Meg,' said Daisy, wriggling herself back in her chair. She looked adoringly at Cici. Daisy loved Cici because she was so funny. She made all the kids laugh.

Eventually Charlie bribed her sister with a promise of a story later, if she left.

'You can see why we don't have Sassy Sister meetings here very often,' said Charlie. 'It's just too *noisy*.'

'Try living in a caravan with Harry the Wizard, Bella the Dinosaur and Summer the Wicked,' I said.

I was thinking back to this morning when I was getting ready for school. Mum had left early for work and Papa was making us breakfast in the cottage. When my grandmother,

Mimi, came to check on us, Bella was chasing Summer around the caravan with her dinosaur tail on. Harry was still in his pyjamas, making a plastic cockroach appear and disappear from behind my ear. Summer barked, Bella bellowed, and Harry bawled, 'Alakazam!' in his best magician voice. Mimi put her hands over her ears and shuddered theatrically.

Charlie pulled a wry face at me. We both knew all about rowdy siblings.

'It won't be long now until Pippa's tower room is ready,' Cici reminded us. 'Then we will have somewhere quiet and peaceful to go.'

'It could still take ages,' I said, a little gloomily. 'The builders have only just finished the upstairs kitchen. Now they have to do all the bedrooms. The tower room will be the very last thing they finish.'

Our builders were turning the upstairs of the cafe into an apartment for us to live in. The tower room was a tiny, round room with glorious views over Kira Cove, which could only be reached from a narrow staircase hidden in my bedroom cupboard. We were all longing for the day when we could use it as our secret Sassy Sisters meeting place.

Oscar began practising his trumpet in the living room. The music blared through the open door. Trixie twitched her whiskers, jumped off my lap and stalked out of the room. I love the way cats can be so very haughty. You know exactly what they are thinking.

'Oscar,' cried Charlie in despair. 'Can't you practise later?'

Oscar yelled back, 'I'm rehearsing for the talent quest. The auditions are on Tuesday, so I don't have much time.'

Our principal, Mrs Black, had announced this morning that Kira Cove School would be holding a talent quest. The auditions would be open to all students, and the best five acts would get to perform for a special group of VIP guests (that is, Very Important People!) who were coming to visit from the mainland. We were all super-curious to know whose these VIP guests could be.

Oscar gave another long blast on his trumpet. Charlie covered her ears.

'Why don't we go outside?' suggested Meg. 'We can visit Archie and Clementine.'

Archie and Clementine were Charlie's donkeys. We all jumped to our feet with relief at this suggestion and raced out the back door. The two dogs chased after us.

I love visiting Charlie's place because it's like being on a mini farm. To the left of the garden is a vegetable patch (well-fenced to stop the animals getting in). Then there is a small orchard of orange, lime and lemon trees where the five chickens scratch around.

At the very back of the property is a grassy paddock with a huge old mango tree. It has an open stable where Maisie the lamb and the two donkeys live.

We raced over to the paddock. Archie and Clementine trotted up to the fence to greet us. Charlie unlatched the gate and we went in.

'Make sure you latch the gate properly,' said Charlie. 'Clementine is the trickiest escape artist.'

'I remember you telling us about the time all the animals broke into your kitchen, Charlie,' I said. 'Maisie tried to eat the board game.'

We all giggled.

Charlie scratched Clementine behind the ear. Clementine leaned her head against Charlie's chest affectionately. Archie came up on the other side and rubbed his cheek against her arm.

We all made a fuss of the two donkeys and then Maisie the lamb galloped up, hoping for a bottle of milk.

Charlie opened the tack room attached to the stable. This is where the saddles, bridles, halters and animal feed were stored. The room smelled of old leather, linseed oil and sweet, dusty chaff. We pulled out four prickly hay bales and sat down. It was blissfully quiet.

Maisie, Zorro and Bandit curled up together on the floor. I'm sure Maisie thought she was a dog too. They looked so cute that I doodled a picture of them in the margin of my notebook. I felt happy and content hanging out with my friends with the whole weekend stretching before us. That was until Cici came up with her not-so-brilliant idea.

'I think we should enter the talent quest,' she announced. 'We could do something amazing and be chosen to perform for the special guests!'

'I would *love* that,' said Charlie, sitting up straight, her green eyes sparkling. 'We could pick one of our favourite songs and work out a dance routine.'

'A dance routine?' I squeaked, dropping my pen. 'I'll never learn a whole dance by Tuesday!'

Dancing was not one of my strong points. We had been doing dance with Miss Demi for weeks now and I was only just starting to remember the choreography for that. I had been doing extra practice at home and with the girls, but I still wasn't confident.

Cici pulled a funny face, clearly remembering some of my dance moves. 'Maybe not.'

'What about reciting a poem or a scene from a play?' suggested Meg.

I rolled my eyes in horror. I definitely didn't want to recite either. I wasn't at all keen to audition. The thought of getting up in front of the whole school and performing made me feel squeamish. While I was happy to be involved in fun group activities like our school newspaper, I really *hated* getting up on stage and being the centre of attention.

I remembered back to a school play we did in London when I was in year three. I had had such bad stage fright that I simply couldn't say my lines. All I could think about was the audience staring at me while I gawped wordlessly like a goldfish. It was one of the most humiliating experiences of my life and I was in no hurry to repeat it.

'I know,' said Charlie. 'We could sing one of our favourite songs. One that we all know and love!'

Charlie was super-excited about the talent quest, I could tell. Her whole face was alight with enthusiasm. Well, clearly Charlie had never heard of stage fright.

'Or not,' I said. 'We don't need to enter the talent quest. Let's leave the performing to the drama queens of the world. Like Olivia.'

Meg shot me a reproachful look. Meg hates it if she thinks I'm sniping at Olivia.

'Come on, Pippa,' said Cici. 'Don't be a spoilsport. Charlie and I can play the guitar and we can all sing.'

'It'll be fun,' said Charlie. 'You sang with us at the Beach Shack at Ruby's farewell.'

'That was different,' I said. 'I didn't know Ruby was going to ask us, so I didn't have time to feel nervous. Besides, everyone was focusing on Ruby, not us. And we weren't in front of a group of VIP guests.'

'We might not even get chosen,' said Meg, a little hopefully, I thought. 'Let's just try out for the audition and see what happens.'

'Why don't you three do it without me?' I suggested. 'You are much better singers than me. I don't have a musical bone in my body.'

'Come on,' said Charlie. 'You can sing! And it will be much more fun if we all do it together.'

'It could be a Sassy Sisters project,' wheedled Cici. She said it as though she was offering me a delicious sweet treat.

I looked around at my three friends. Charlie's face was glowing with excitement. Cici was bubbling with anticipation. Meg wasn't a super-keen performer but she was the peacemaker of our group, so of course she wanted me to say yes too.

The downside of being in a group of friends is that sometimes you feel pressured into doing things you don't really want to do. Like singing in a talent quest!

I sighed. 'All right, I'll do it.'

'Great,' said Charlie, giving me a hug. 'We can sing "Kira Dreaming". We all know that one, and Cici and I have been learning it at guitar lessons.'

'Kira Dreaming' was the song that Ruby Starr had performed for the very first time at her farewell bash a couple of weeks ago. It was a catchy song about treasuring friendship and chasing your dreams. Ruby said she was inspired to write it after hearing Charlie singing one of her songs on the beach at Kira Cove.

Ever since Ruby performed it at the opening night of her world tour, we've heard it played over and over again – on the radio, in shops and on the builders' music player. I even thought I'd heard our neighbour, Mrs Beecham, humming it once but when I asked her she flatly denied it.

'We'll need to work out costumes and props,' said Charlie. 'Something that suits the song and grabs people's attention.'

'Maybe Meg and Pippa could play a percussion instrument like a tambourine or a bongo drum,' suggested Cici. 'That would add some extra energy to our act.'

The girls started discussing ideas for costumes and props. I crossed my arms stubbornly and said nothing. First the girls wanted me to get up on stage and sing, and now they want me to get dressed up in a silly costume and bang a drum. This idea was getting worse and worse.

'The song has a beachy vibe, so we could wear board shorts and singlets, or wetsuits,' said Meg. 'We could even use surfboards as a backdrop.'

Wetsuits on stage! I thought to myself. *We'd look ridiculous! Everyone will laugh at us.*

'Or long boho skirts with flower crowns?' suggested Charlie.

'I was thinking something more glamorous,' said Cici. 'Like evening dresses, all glittery and sparkly. Or maybe we go totally fun and crazy, like tutus, tiaras and stripy leggings.'

'Where would we get evening dresses by Tuesday?' I asked, grumpily. 'Or crazy tutus for that matter?'

Charlie looked at me with disappointment. 'Maybe we could make something?'

I huffed with impatience.

Cici glared at me. 'Maybe you could just *pretend* to be enthusiastic, Pippa?' said Cici. 'We won't have a chance in the talent quest unless we all give it our best shot.'

I felt a flash of guilt. Friendships can be very complicated sometimes.

CHAPTER 2

MYSTERY THIEF

Charlie fetched her guitar from the house, together with the music and lyrics. Cici played an air guitar, practising her chords.

'Okay,' said Charlie. 'One, two, three . . .' She began to strum the opening notes.

Charlie had a lovely voice – sweet and clear. Cici sang enthusiastically. Meg and I didn't know all the words, so we leaned over Charlie's shoulder to read them. I sang softly, missing half the lyrics, but the others didn't sound too bad.

That was until Zorro and Bandit decided to join in, howling along with the music. This distracted Charlie so she started to make mistakes, stumbling over a few chords.

Clementine and Archie stuck their heads through the door to find out what all the racket was. Maisie gambolled away as fast as she could. I didn't blame her.

A moment later Seb, Oscar and Sophia popped their heads around the door.

'You guys sound like you're being strangled,' said Oscar, helpfully. 'Maybe you should choose a different song.'

Zorro and Bandit howled louder. Seb pretended to conduct the music with two fingers.

'Thanks, Oscar,' said Charlie, with a touch of sarcasm. 'Says the boy whose trumpet sounds like fingernails on a chalkboard. Why don't you go and practise your own piece?'

'Good point,' said Seb, with a broad grin on his face. 'Maybe Zorro and Bandit can come to school and perform for both your acts. Their howling would only be an improvement!'

'*Go!*' commanded Charlie, shooing them away with her hand.

Oscar waggled his fingers in farewell and they all ran off. I checked my watch.

'I have to go too,' I said, pretending to be upset. 'It's nearly five o'clock and I promised Mum I'd be back in time to help clean up.'

I often helped Mum and our barista, Zoe, at the cafe after closing time on Friday afternoons. Mum paid me some pocket money to clear the tables, wash up and do any odd jobs.

'Okay,' said Cici, 'but we still need to do lots of practice over the weekend.'

'Somewhere quiet where we won't bother anyone,' said Charlie. 'Or be bothered. So clearly my place is out!'

'You could come to our yacht,' said Meg doubtfully. 'But it's a bit squishy for all of us with Mum, Dad and Jack there.'

Cici looked at me with raised eyebrows. Clearly she hadn't quite forgiven me for my lack of enthusiasm.

'The caravan's no good either,' I said. 'But perhaps we could rehearse upstairs, above the cafe. The builders won't be there on a Saturday, and we shouldn't disturb the customers if we close the door.'

Cici smiled at me. 'Perfect. Let's meet at ten o'clock at the Beach Shack.'

The three of us said goodbye to Charlie and her family, and set off to walk back down to the cove. A long flight of steep stone steps led from the plateau, down to the beachfront of Kira Cove. The steps were shaded with tall mango trees, palms and a riot of hot-pink bougainvillea vines. We walked on the paved esplanade towards our cafe.

As we strolled along we saw a group of girls practising gymnastics on the lawn that ran beside the path.

There were five of them doing a complicated routine that involved lots of somersaults,
backflips, splits and cartwheels. All five of
them rolled around in a perfect circle.

As we came closer I recognised them. It
was Olivia Gray and a group of girls from
our class – Tash, Willow, Sienna and Jemila.
They were wearing matching purple-and-black
leotards and had perfect high ponytails. Tash
broke out of the circle and cartwheeled right
over to us on the path.

'Hi, girls,' she said, then kept cartwheeling
back onto the grass. Tash was an outstanding
gymnast and could do sixty-seven cartwheels
in a row. Sometimes I thought she was happiest
when she was upside down.

Olivia landed gracefully on her feet and
walked over to us. The other girls crowded
around too.

'What are you guys up to?' asked Cici curi-
ously. 'You don't normally do gym on Friday
afternoons.'

'We're practising for the talent quest auditions,' explained Olivia. 'We've been working on a new routine at gymnastics for the last couple of weeks, so we want to make sure we can all remember it.'

'Normally we practise in the gym at school with music,' said Sienna. 'But the hip-hop class is in there on Friday, so we thought we'd just practise on the grass.'

The girls didn't look like they needed any practice to me. Their routine was perfect. Maybe that was a good thing. If the gym girls had an amazing routine then we were less likely to be chosen for the VIP performance.

'You all look brilliant,' I said. 'I think the judges will love it.'

'Thanks,' said Tash, beaming at me. 'We want to do really well. Our teacher, Miss Ashleigh, thinks if we keep working hard, we could go and compete at the regional championships on the mainland.'

'What about you guys?' asked Willow. 'Are you going to enter the quest?'

Cici glanced at Meg and me. 'We'd like to. But we haven't quite worked everything out yet.'

'We'd better get back to it,' said Olivia. 'We've only got until Tuesday to get it perfect.'

Cici, Meg and I waved goodbye and walked on until I peeled off at the Beach Shack.

'See you tomorrow at ten,' said Cici. 'I'll bring my guitar.'

'Hi, Pippa,' called Zoe, as I walked through the front door. She was making a ham-and-brie sandwich at the kitchen bench.

Zoe was our red-haired barista from Sydney, who was staying on Kira Island for a working holiday before she started university. She smiled at me and wiped her hands on a tea towel. 'Your Mum's just taken the mail to the postbox.'

'Hi, Zoe,' I replied. 'Would you like me to clear the tables?'

As I spoke I thought I saw something move in the shadows under the tables to my left. I looked again but there was nothing there. It must have been my imagination playing tricks on me.

'That would be great. Thanks, Pippa,' said Zoe, cutting her sandwich in half. 'It's been so busy today I've hardly had time to eat anything. Would you like something?'

'No, thanks,' I replied. 'We ate at Charlie's house.'

Zoe carried her plate over to a table next to the long window seat that ran along the wall. Just then the phone rang and Zoe dashed to answer it.

'Hello, the Beach Shack Cafe. Zoe speaking. Can I help you?' she said in her bright, friendly voice. Zoe paused, listening to the person on the other end. 'No. I'm sorry. Jenna's not here now. Can I take a message? No? Okay. Well, she should be back in a few minutes. Goodbye.'

I began clearing up in the bookstore part of the cafe. There were several low coffee tables and comfy armchairs with plump feather cushions. The tables were crammed with dirty teacups, side plates and a teapot covered in roses. I carried them to the sink then went back to wipe down the tables.

Zoe poured herself a glass of pineapple juice and took it over to her table by the window. She stopped and looked down then all around.

'Pippa. Did you take half my sandwich?' she asked with a puzzled tone.

'No,' I said. I came over and stood beside Zoe. On the table was the apple-green plate with half a sandwich on it. The other piece was gone.

'I put my sandwich down on the table, went to answer the phone and now half of it's disappeared,' said Zoe. We both looked around the cafe. There was no one there.

'Maybe a seagull came in and stole it?' I suggested. The seagulls could be a nuisance. They often hung around the jetty, stealing scraps and leftovers.

'Could a seagull fly off with half a sandwich?' asked Zoe. 'Maybe a crust but not the whole thing. And I didn't see any gulls come in.'

I shrugged and picked up a small piece of brie that had fallen on the window seat.

Zoe sighed and cleared away the remaining sandwich. 'I'm not that hungry anyway.'

I carried the empty milk bottles outside to throw in the recycling bin. Beside the bins was a stack of timber fruit crates. Our fruit and vegetables were delivered from the mainland in timber crates to protect them on the ferry crossing. I picked up one of the crates. It was rustic, but felt strong and sturdy. My mind started ticking over as I wondered whether

I could make something useful with these crates. I had seen a photo in one of Mum's design magazines of display shelves made from old boxes. Maybe I could do something similar.

Just then Mum arrived with Bella and Harry.

'Mum, do you think I could use some of these wooden crates?' I asked. 'I have a project they might be good for.'

'Sure, Pipkin,' she said, giving me a hug. 'Are you making something for school?'

I was about to explain my idea to Mum when Bella interrupted.

'Did you hear there's going to be a talent quest, Pippa?' asked Bella. 'I'm going to sing a song, all by myself. I'm going to wear my dinosaur suit and sing the dinosaur romp.'

Bella opened her mouth wide and began to bellow, miming the actions as she sang.

'Crash. Crash. Stomp your feet.
Gnash. Gnash. Bare your teeth.

Chomp. Chomp. Slash your claws.
Dance the dinosaur romp. ROARRRR!'

I put my hands over my ears. It was truly terrible. Harry and I exchanged dismayed glances.

Bella danced away through the cafe, stomping, gnashing and chomping at the top of her voice.

I looked at Mum in horror. 'Mum, she can't. You can't let her do that in public!'

Mum looked rather worried. 'Well, Bella-boo is rather a performer. With the background music playing and a costume, I'm sure she'll be adorable.'

So it looked like the talent quest was going to be humiliating on several fronts. Not only was I going to be mortified when Olivia and her gang gave a stellar gymnastic performance while our singing was awful, but now I was going to have my sister the *Tyrannosaurus rex* terrify the whole school.

Harry helped me stack the dishwasher, while Zoe cleaned the coffee machine. Mum emptied the cash register and tallied up the receipts.

I grabbed the broom and began to sweep the floor. Under the window seat in the shadows, I discovered a mess. There were two half-slices of mangled bread and a smudge of soggy brie. I fetched the dustpan and broom to sweep it up.

'Yuck,' I said to Zoe as I dropped the mess in the bin. 'Some people are disgusting! Who'd throw their sandwich scraps on the floor of the cafe?'

Zoe shook her head in disbelief. 'You wouldn't believe the bad manners of some of them. Most of our customers are lovely but when I worked at the cafe back in Sydney, I met some absolute horrors.'

When everything was clean and tidy, Zoe said goodbye, grabbed her bike and cycled home to her flat. Mum locked up and then the four of us walked home along the beach to Mimi and Papa's. I always loved this walk – breathing the salty air and hearing the sound of the waves crashing on the sand. Kira Beach must be one of the most stunning beaches in the world. As we walked we called hello to lots of people we knew. Many of them were customers at the cafe.

Mimi and Papa's cottage is half-hidden by a lush tropical garden of frangipanis, hibiscus and palm trees with a curling wisteria vine dangling purple flowers over the front veranda. Our caravan is parked out the back. Mum went inside the caravan to start making dinner. Bella went to help Mimi feed the chooks. Harry and I went inside the cottage to fetch Summer the Wicked. Harry brought a bundle of paper clutched in his hand.

Our twelve-week-old puppy galloped towards us as soon as we opened the back door. Mimi and Papa look after Summer while Mum is at work and we're at school. Anyone would think we'd been away for six months instead of just a few hours. She was so excited – yipping and whining with relief that we were back.

We'd finally trained her not to jump up on us, so she gambolled around in circles instead, chasing her tail. She raced faster and faster, around and around, until she fell over her own feet, rolling on her back with her paws in the air.

We all laughed and I scratched Summer on the tummy. 'She's been sleeping all afternoon, so now she's bursting with energy,' said Papa. 'You'd better take her for a run.'

Harry waved his bundle of paper around. 'Papa, I was wondering if you could help me, please? In the work shed? I have a special project I need to do.'

'What is it?' I asked Harry, trying to see what was printed on the paper. It looked like some sort of building plan.

'Just something for school,' he said, as he folded the paper in half so I couldn't see.

'Sure, Harry,' said Papa. 'I'd love to help.' The two of them headed out to Papa's work shed in the back garden.

'Come on, Summer,' I called, as we raced into the back garden. 'Let's play.'

Summer still wasn't allowed to go outside the garden just in case she met another dog who could make her sick. Our vet, Caitlin, who is Willow's mum, had said she couldn't go outside the garden until a few days after her third vaccination, just to be safe.

I threw the ball for Summer to chase. I ran so she could chase me. We played tug-of-war with her rope toy. Then, when Summer had burned up some energy, we started our training.

'Summer, come,' I called. Summer raced to my foot and plonked down on her bottom.

She was much better behaved now. Most of the time she would walk to heel, sit on command and come when she was called. Although she was still super-naughty at times and had an absolute passion for chewing shoes. Harry, Bella and I had all become very good at putting our things away, otherwise they ended up gobbled. Mum wouldn't let us get too cross with Summer because she said it was our fault if we left our things lying around where a puppy could eat them.

Despite her wickedness, we all loved having our very own puppy. I'd wanted a dog for years back in London, but it had still been a surprise just how much fun it was have an animal of your very own to play with and look after.

I clipped Summer's red lead onto her collar.

'Summer, walk on,' I commanded. At first Summer tried to fight the lead – chewing it and tangling herself up until she was like a Christmas present tied with ribbon. I made her sit. Once she was untangled we started again.

This time she did it properly, walking perfectly at my heel as we circled the garden. As we worked on her sit, stay and come commands, I could hear sounds of sawing and hammering coming from Papa's work shed. From the caravan I could hear the sound of Bella roaring out the words to her dino romp song. I had the feeling it was going to be a very long weekend.

CHAPTER 3

A FLOWER-THROWING POLTERGEIST

Normally I liked to sleep in on Saturday mornings, but I was woken bright and early by Bella digging around in the cupboard. Bella's favourite dress-up costume was a green dinosaur tail, but she also had another one that she only wore on special occasions. It was a furry green dinosaur onesie with claws on the hands and feet, a long tail which swept along the ground and a hood with a ferocious-looking dinosaur head on it. It was too hot to wear in the tropical heat of Kira Island, which is why it was mostly packed away in the bottom of the cupboard.

Bella clambered into it and began humming her new favourite song. I decided it might be best to escape to the cafe with Mum.

When we left, Harry was busy with Papa in the work shed and Mimi was looking after Bella. It was nice to have Mum all to myself as we walked along the beachfront in the fresh morning air. We chatted about what had been happening at school and I told Mum about my afternoon at Charlie's yesterday.

'I can't wait until the tower room's ready and we can meet there,' I said.

'It won't be too much longer,' said Mum. 'The builders have fixed the floor up there now and the roof doesn't leak anymore.'

'Does that mean the builders are nearly finished? Can we move in soon?' I asked with great excitement. I couldn't wait to have my own room again.

'Sorry, Pipkin,' said Mum. 'Not quite. The builders still have a few weeks' work. And then we have to paint it all.'

'Oh,' I said, drooping with disappointment. We'd painted the downstairs cafe with Mimi and Papa's help and it had taken ages. Upstairs would take even longer because there were so many more walls.

'Mimi and Papa are going to help us start painting tomorrow. It should only take a few weekends to get it all done.'

A few weekends? That could mean months!

Mum's phone rang as we arrived at the cafe. She checked the caller name and pulled a little face. For a moment she looked sad, then she squeezed me tight.

'I think I'll deal with that later,' she said, as she switched the phone off.

Mum unlocked the front door to the cafe and we went inside. But instead of the beautifully clean cafe that we had left last night, someone or something had made a mega-mess.

Cushions had tumbled from the window seat to the floor. A small vase had been knocked over and the roses were scattered along the refectory table, leaving puddles of water.

'Goodness me,' said Mum. 'Whatever could have happened here?'

Zoe arrived and joined us. We all stood in the centre of the cafe, staring at the mess.

'I hope the table's not ruined,' wailed Mum. Papa had built her a beautiful table out of hundred-year-old timber as a cafe-warming present. Zoe, Mum and I began mopping up the spillage on the table top. Zoe gathered up the wilting flowers and put them back in the vase. I replaced the cushions.

'Do you think someone could have broken in?' asked Zoe, as she filled the vase with fresh water from the sink. Mum checked all the doors and windows, looking worried.

'No. Everything's safely locked.'

'Perhaps we have a resident ghost,' joked Zoe. 'A poltergeist who enjoys throwing flowers around!'

Mum and I laughed. Then we forgot about it as the first of the day's customers arrived. It was Nigel, the Kira Beach lifesaver, picking up some coffee and a banana muffin on his way to work. He grinned at me. 'And when are you joining my surf lifesaving patrol, young lady!'

Nigel said this every time he saw me, ever since I'd helped Meg and Jack rescue a young family who had been swept into a rip. I grinned back at him and told him I could start tomorrow.

The girls arrived at about ten o'clock, Charlie and Cici both carrying their guitars. After saying hello, we went upstairs. As always, the girls were keen to see what progress our builders, Jason, Dan and Miguel, had made during the week.

The living room and kitchen was a large open-plan area, with sliding windows that opened onto a veranda overlooking the cove.

This room was now finished, except for the unpainted walls and the missing appliances. The kitchen had a teal-blue tiled splashback, a pale-grey benchtop and glistening white cupboards with gaps for the oven, dishwasher and fridge.

'We're going to start painting tomorrow,' I said.

'What colour?' asked Charlie.

'Mum's chosen a coral-white because she says that will set off the blues of the view.'

Mum had everything for the painting project stacked in the corner. There was a pile of neatly folded drop sheets, paint tins, clean brushes, rollers and paint trays.

We checked all the other rooms, then finished up in my bedroom.

'Ooh,' said Cici. 'They've built your window seat.'

The girls raced over and sat down on it. There were no cushions yet but it was a perfect place to sit and read or draw or just admire the gorgeous views out the window. I was rather proud of my window seat, as I had designed it myself based on a photo I'd seen in a magazine. It had deep drawers underneath it to store all my treasures and was extra wide.

On the wall was my mood board where I'd stuck up magazine photos, images from the internet and a collection of my doodles and designs. There were lots of gorgeous beachy rooms in shades of turquoise, sea-green and white. The mood board was Cici's brilliant suggestion so I could create my perfect bedroom.

'And the new bookshelves look great,' added Meg, taking a closer look.

'All my books from London are packed away in boxes in storage,' I said. 'It will be really cool to unpack all my things and set them up.'

On the left side of the window seat were floor-to-ceiling bookshelves, still empty, of course. On the right side was a set of built-in cupboards. This was one of the best things about my room. Inside the cupboard were all the usual things like shelves, drawers and hanging space. But there was also a secret – a narrow ladder that led upstairs to the tower room above.

Charlie and Cici pulled out their guitars from their cases and began to strum, perching on the edge of the window seat.

Charlie had brought us all a photocopy of the music and lyrics, so we began to sing.

Charlie made us sing 'Kira Dreaming' over and over again.

'It's not quite right,' said Charlie. 'Maybe if we play and sing along to the real song, we can copy how Ruby does it.'

I set up the builders' music player and started playing the recorded version. We sang along to it at least another ten times over the next half an hour. We sang until I was sick of the sound of it.

'Let's take a little break,' said Charlie, shaking her stiff hands. 'My fingers are aching.'

We all stood up and stretched. Cici put down her guitar and began examining the photos and doodles on my mood board. Meg looked out the window.

'I think I can see the dolphins,' she said, craning her neck. 'Shall we go upstairs to see if we can get a better view?'

'Sure,' I said. I loved watching the Kira Cove dolphins surfing and playing.

I opened the cupboard door. We scrambled up the ladder one by one, popping out in the round tower room above. Large rectangular windows looked out in all directions. We stood there, searching the waves for a sign of the dolphin pod. But either Meg had been mistaken or they had disappeared underwater.

Cici turned her attention to the walls of the tower room. They were old timber planks, grey with age. The builders had patched a couple of holes in the walls and floor with pale yellow plaster. The ceiling was low and sloping, coming down to just above the windows, and was spotted with black mould and brown watermarks. It all looked rather shabby.

'I've been thinking,' said Cici, with that mischievous look she gets when she's scheming. I hoped this wasn't going to be another of Cici's harebrained ideas – like singing in the talent quest. She looked around at us all. 'Maybe we should paint the tower room ourselves. Instead of waiting for the builders to finish everything else.'

Now this was more like it. I grinned at Cici. 'That's a brilliant idea. Mum has the paint and brushes all ready to go.'

Charlie ran her fingertips over the rough, splintery timber.

'The tower room's not very big, so it shouldn't take very long,' she said.

'Then we could clean all the windows,' said Meg. 'And furnish it with bits and pieces we get from home.'

'I'm sure Mum has some old cushions we could use,' said Cici. 'I'll ask her.'

I felt a thrill of excitement as I thought about the four of us working together to make the tower room a beautiful space for us to meet.

'Let's do it,' I said. 'We can start right now. I'll go and ask Mum if it's okay.'

I scrambled down the ladder and went downstairs to the cafe.

Mum was making up lunch platters for a big group of people who were celebrating a birthday. She looked busy, so I didn't want to disturb her. Besides, I was secretly worried that if Mum saw me she might start giving me jobs to do! I snuck back upstairs. Perhaps it was better to do it as a surprise. Besides, Papa had shown me how to paint when we were doing the bookcases in the cafe. How hard could it be?

'Let's get started,' I said.

We hadn't planned to paint, so none of us were wearing old clothes. We'd just need to be extra careful. We lugged the rollers, brushes and trays up the ladder, then a tin of paint, which was rather tricky because it was surprisingly heavy.

I remembered to stir the paint, then we poured it into one of the trays. A bit too much paint rushed out, splashing on the floor. I used a paint brush to mop it up.

Charlie started slathering paint on the middle of the wall, using the roller.

'I think we're meant to do the edges first,' said Meg, carefully running her brush along the bottom edge of a window.

Cici chose another window to edge. I started painting the bottom edge where the wall met the floor. I tried to be careful but it was actually quite tricky to stop the brush from streaking the floor as well. We couldn't reach up very high, so we just painted as far as we could standing on tippy-toes – most of the way up the walls between the windows. We couldn't quite reach the sloping ceiling.

Charlie sang as we worked.

'Not that song,' I begged. 'Can't you sing something different?'

'We should all be singing it while we paint,' suggested Charlie, slathering more paint on the round wall. The roller filled in a large area quite quickly. The room was being transformed.

I stepped back to admire our handiwork – straight into the half-full paint tray. The tray flipped up and flicked paint everywhere.

'Pippa!' yelled Meg, Cici and Charlie all together. The girls were splattered. I was splattered. And there were specks of paint on the windows, the floor and the walls. I jumped out of the paint tray, smudging white foot prints on the floor.

'Don't move,' said Cici. 'You'll make it worse.'

I stared around in dismay. Our great idea of painting the tower room wasn't going so well. Meg used her brush to transfer some of the spilled paint from the floor to the wall.

'We need some rags,' said Charlie. 'I'd better go. You'll walk paint marks everywhere.'

'Maybe down in the kitchen,' I suggested.

Charlie climbed down the ladder. Cici and Meg kept brushing up spilled paint and spreading it on the walls to use it up.

A few minutes later Charlie returned with a handful of rags and Mum.

Mum looked around in disbelief. 'Oh, girls.'

Cici, Meg and Charlie all smiled hopefully at Mum.

'Hi, Jenna,' said Meg.

'We thought we'd give Pippa a hand painting,' explained Cici.

'I can see that,' said Mum, rubbing her forehead. 'What a terrible mess.'

Here we go, I thought. *We are going to get into super-huge trouble.*

'We'll clean it all up, Mum,' I said anxiously, looking around at the chaos. 'We just wanted to make it look fresh and beautiful. But . . . it was a bit harder than I thought.'

'Next time, make sure you ask me before you start work on one of your projects, Pipkin. Even if I am busy,' said Mum.

'Sorry, Mum,' I said.

Mum gave me a kiss on the forehead, which may have been the only clean spot on my body.

'I guess it could have been much worse,' she said. 'But I think we're going to have to paint this whole floor white to hide the evidence!'

Meg fetched some water and the four of us set to work to clean up the spilled paint. We wiped the speckles off our bodies and from our hair. There wasn't much we could do about the paint on our clothes or the floor.

When everything was packed away we

examined our work. I'd had visions of a gorgeous space, in a glistening fresh, coral-white. Instead the paint looked patchy and sparse. More greyish than white, with huge splodges on the floor, the top half still unpainted and the windows salt-smeared and speckled with paint drops.

'It looks worse,' I said. All my excitement had evaporated, leaving me feeling totally dejected. Cici gave me a hug.

'Another coat will make it look much better,' she promised.

I just hoped she was right!

CHAPTER 4

SUMMER'S RUMPUS

Sunday was Mum's official painting day. We headed to the cafe early, straight after breakfast. This time I was wearing my oldest, grottiest clothes with a cap to cover my hair.

Mimi and Papa were coming for the day to help us. Papa had packed the station wagon with more paint brushes, more paint tins and some long-handled rollers. But when Harry, Bella and I arrived at the car, Mum had a surprise for us.

Summer was sitting beside the car, with her red lead clipped on and her pink tongue sticking out. She thumped her plumed tail on the ground in welcome.

'Is Summer coming with us?' I asked, fondling her ears. Summer hadn't been out with us except for her trips to visit Caitlin the vet.

'Today is a special day for Summer,' said Mum. 'It's time she ventured out into the big wide world.'

I skipped with delight. I suddenly realised that it was a few days since Summer had her last injection.

'I thought you and Harry might like to walk her down to the cafe while we drive,' said Mum.

'*Yes*,' said Harry and I together.

'What about me?' demanded Bella.

'You can come with us,' said Mum, soothingly. 'We need to start work on the painting and you're a great helper.'

'But I want to walk with Summer,' said Bella crossly. 'I don't want to go in the car like a baby. I'm a big kid now.'

Mum looked closely at Harry, Bella and me. The walk down to the cafe was really easy. There was only one quiet street to cross before you were on the esplanade – the wide pathway and parkland that runs all the way along the beach down to Kira Cove.

Mum gave Bella a tight squeeze. 'All right, Bella-boo. But Pipkin's the eldest, so she has to hold Summer's lead all the way. And I want you to walk straight down to the cafe. Don't get distracted.'

'Sure, Mum. We'll be fine,' I said, keen to get away. How hard could it be?

Just then Mum's phone rang. She checked the caller name on the screen. Mum frowned, looking upset.

'I won't take this now,' she said, putting the phone back in her pocket. 'We have far too much to do today. Let's go.'

Mum helped us make sure Summer crossed the street safely.

'I nearly forgot,' said Mum, waving a black plastic bag at us. 'Here's a bag in case she does a poo along the way. Make sure you pick it up and put it in the bin.'

'Yuck,' said Bella. 'Not me. That can be Pippa's job. She's the *eldest*!'

I rolled my eyes at Bella and took the poo bag, knotting it to the end of the lead.

Mum jumped in the car with Mimi and Papa. They tooted the horn and waved us off. We crossed the park and then we were on the beachfront. As always, the esplanade was busy with kids riding bikes, couples strolling and surfers carrying their boards. A family on scooters raced past, dodging around us. On the sand, two teams of teenagers were playing a rowdy game of beach volleyball.

Summer bounded along with excitement, her nose to the ground snuffling all the delightful new smells. She zigzagged back and forth, sniffing light poles, tree trunks and tussocks of grass. Her tail wagged madly. I had to run to keep up with her. Harry and Bella ran along beside us.

'Slow down, girl,' cried Bella, clutching her side. 'I'm puffed.'

Suddenly Summer came to a dead stop. A palm frond had fallen on the path. Summer eyed it cautiously. She sniffed it. When it didn't bite, she pounced. She grabbed the frond with her teeth and dragged it along the esplanade. The palm frond was over a metre long – nearly four times the length of our chubby puppy!

'Leave it, Summer,' I suggested, but Summer was having too much fun. She insisted on dragging her new toy behind her, super-proud of her special treasure. At last she abandoned the palm frond, but only because she had spotted something far more exciting. On the side of the path was a flowerbed of bright orange marigolds, their heads nodding in the breeze.

In a single bound, Summer had her nose buried among the flowers, sniffing and nipping. She stole the heads off several flowers and flopped down to chomp them.

'She's eating the flowers,' shrieked Bella.

'Naughty girl,' I scolded, pulling the mangled petals from her mouth. 'Stop chewing everything in sight.'

'Come on, girl,' coaxed Harry.

For a moment, I thought Summer would never be persuaded to leave her delicious snack. Then she caught sight of something really amazing. In a split second she was off and racing. In the distance was . . . another dog! Summer bounded forward, dragging me along behind her. Who'd have thought a puppy could be so strong!

Suddenly I recognised her target. The dog was wrinkly-faced with brown fur, darker ears and a black nose. It was Cici's puggle, Muffin. Holding onto Muffin's lead was Cici, gliding along on her skateboard. She was looking gorgeous in aqua shorts covered in roses, a white singlet top and white runners.

'Hi, Cici,' I called, tugging on Summer's lead as we slid to a stop beside her. Summer dropped down on all fours, with her bottom stuck up in the air, while she waited to see what Muffin would do. Muffin ignored her.

'Summer's out walking at last,' said Cici, giving her a pat. But Summer wasn't interested in Cici. She had eyes only for Muffin.

Muffin glanced at Summer and our pup went crazy. She licked Muffin all over her face, jumping around like a pogo stick. She rolled on her back and stuck her paws in the air submissively. Then she bounded up and did her demented ballerina routine, pirouetting at top speed.

Muffin looked away and yawned, appearing to be extremely bored by the antics of a playful puppy. Summer tilted her head to the side, her ears cocked, then she pawed Muffin, begging for attention. We all giggled.

'Summer can't understand why Muffin's not as crazy about her as she is about Muffin,' I said.

'They'll be good friends once they get to know each other,' said Cici, stroking Summer's silky back.

We began walking together towards the cafe, Cici carrying her skateboard. Or at least we walked and Summer bounded, her golden ears flapping up and down like bird's wings. She was far too excited to walk to heel despite my constant reminders. She kept licking Muffin on the nose as if checking she was still there.

There were lots of dogs out walking that morning. Summer went through the same wild welcome for each one. And every dog walker wanted to fondle and fuss over our adorable pup. It took forever!

Then, halfway along the beach, Summer completely ran out of battery. All that exercise was far too much for her and she collapsed in the middle of the path.

'Poor puppy,' cooed Harry. 'She's tired.'

'Come on, Summer,' I begged, tugging on the lead. She closed her eyes and sprawled in the sunshine, like a puddle of coral sand. No cajoling would get her to move. There was nothing for me to do but pick her up and carry her in my arms.

'She's so heavy,' I complained with a huff.

'She must weigh ten kilos by now,' said Harry. That didn't sound like very much, but when you have to lug a puppy along the beach in the hot Kira sunshine it felt like way more than that.

'Muffin looks much happier now she doesn't have her face being licked every ten seconds,' joked Cici. Muffin looked up at Cici and me as if to say 'You bet I am!'.

Cici peeled off to go home, promising to pop by the cafe later that afternoon. Summer opened one eye when Muffin left, then closed it again, too exhausted to move.

Harry and I took turns carrying Summer all the way down the beach. By the time we arrived at the cafe our arms were stiff and sore.

Zoe and her friend Lisa were serving egg-and-bacon rolls to a noisy family of customers at the long table. Mimi was making mugs of tea in the cafe kitchen. 'How was Summer's first walk?' she asked as we trudged through the front door. 'It took a while.'

'She didn't walk at all,' I complained. 'She bounced around like crazy then she was totally unconscious.'

'We had to carry her half the way,' said Harry, as he stroked her nose. Summer snuggled down deeper in Harry's arms. He held her close.

Mimi laughed. 'Your mum put her basket upstairs in the living room. Why don't you take her up?'

Mimi followed us, carrying the tray of tea mugs.

Upstairs Mimi, Papa and Mum had made a great start on painting the living room and kitchen. Papa had a long-handled roller and was filling in the last of the ceiling in flat white. Mum was up a ladder cutting in the edges of the wall colour just below the ceiling.

Harry and I put Summer in her basket out of the way. She woke up for a moment, yawned, showing her pink tongue, then went promptly back to sleep.

Mum and Papa stopped work to sip their tea, while we told them all about Summer's adventures on her first walk. Mimi, Papa and Mum chuckled as we took it in turns to describe Summer's rambunctious activities. Then it was time to get to work. If I thought my arms were tired after carrying Summer up the beach, well, that was nothing compared to how they felt after a few hours of painting!

It took all day to paint the living area. Mum and Papa had stuck masking tape along all the edges so we could get a nice clean line. They had also spread drop sheets all over the floor. I wished I'd remembered to do this when we were painting the tower room. It might have saved a lot of mess.

Harry and I painted along the bottom edge of the wall, while Papa and Mum painted the top edges from the ladder. Bella helped by loading the roller with paint. Mimi used the roller to fill in the wall in between the two lines.

We were so involved in our work that none of us noticed when Summer finally woke up, fresh and full of beans. That is, until she stuck her nose in the paint tin and ended up with a coral-white nose instead of a black one. As much as I tried I couldn't get it all off, so Bella decided to give Summer a total makeover and paint her claws white as well.

At lunchtime we went downstairs to eat. We took Summer down too with her lead on.

Mum made us all ham-cheese-and-tomato toasties with basil. Mimi cut up a platter of icy-cold watermelon. Summer had a small cup of her puppy kibble in a bowl. We ate outside at a shady table on the jetty, enjoying the view. Summer was tied up under the table.

Bella sat on the edge of the jetty, with her plate beside her. She was eating half her toastie and throwing small pieces of crust in the water.

Suddenly Summer started to bark, lunging forward until her lead was strained taut. We all turned to look.

'I wonder what Summer's barking at?' asked Mimi.

Mum shrugged. 'I don't know. Maybe the seagulls. She's never really seen those before.'

Bella turned around to see what Summer was doing, then glanced down at her plate. 'Hey? Where's the rest of my toastie?'

Bella's plate was empty except for a few shreds of basil and some crumbs.

'You must have eaten it without noticing,' said Mum, soothingly.

'No, I didn't,' said Bella, looking extremely put out. 'I ate the first half, then I fed my crust to the fish. Then when I went to eat my second half, it was gone. Did you make it disappear, Harry?'

'How could I have?' asked Harry. 'I was sitting over here eating my own toastie!'

'Maybe you were extra hungry, so you made it disappear by magic,' said Bella. 'You know, like you do with the ball and my coins and Mum's phone.'

'What coins?' asked Papa, trying not to laugh.

'Harry made my pocket money disappear in his magic box,' said Bella. 'And Mum's phone.'

'I brought them back,' said Harry in an injured tone. 'You know I did. But I definitely didn't eat your toastie.'

'Maybe you accidentally fed the whole sandwich to the fish?' suggested Mum, trying to restore the peace. 'Why don't I make you another one?'

I took another bite of my watermelon slice.

'I didn't feed it to the fish,' said Bella. 'But I bet it was Harry who stole it.'

'Harry didn't come anywhere near you, Bella,' I said. 'He couldn't possibly make it magically disappear from the other side of the table.'

'I think it's time to get back to the painting,' suggested Mum. The kids all sighed and huffed and complained but there was nothing for it but to get back to work.

Later in the afternoon, Cici, Charlie and Meg dropped by.

'We've come along to see if we can help,' said Charlie.

'That is, if we're not banned from painting after yesterday,' said Meg, looking sheepishly at Mum.

Mum laughed. 'It's very brave of you to come back and help after the drama of the great paint disaster! But I think you'll do a wonderful job of it today.'

The four of us carried some equipment up into the tower room so we could finish painting. Papa lugged up a stepladder so we could reach the ceiling and top of the walls.

Mum popped up to give us a few tips. She reminded us how to use masking tape to give a straight line on the edges and how to spread a drop sheet to protect the floor. Before heading back downstairs she added, 'And try not to step in the paint tray, Pipkin!'

Then the four of us set to work painting the first coat on the ceiling. I knew now that we should have started with the ceiling and worked down. The four of us chatted while we worked. Charlie even made us practise singing our song while we painted. Personally, I found it hard enough to either paint or sing, without trying to do them both together.

By the time we'd put the first coat on the wall, the ceiling was dry so we could paint that again.

At last we were finished. Then we cleaned all the windows until they sparkled. The four of us stood back and looked around with great pride. To be honest, our paint job was far from perfect, but it was a huge improvement.

'You were right, Cici,' I said. 'It looks amazing.'

'The room somehow looks much bigger now that it's all snowy-white and fresh,' said Charlie.

'Now we can start on the floor,' said Meg, looking down at the dried puddles of white paint on the floorboards. 'If we paint it, you won't see the spills.'

'What do you mean?' asked Cici, with a twinkle in her dark eyes. 'Polka dots are *very* fashionable this season!'

We all giggled, feeling delighted with our achievement.

We grabbed our paintbrushes and started on the floor, working back towards the hole with the ladder down to my room below. I couldn't wait until we could furnish it. I started daydreaming about colourful cushions and shelves.

I had come up with the rather ingenious idea to design some really cool bookshelves that would curve around the round wall of the tower. I could make them myself, using the timber fruit crates from downstairs. I would position them side by side and stack them two or three high, then tie them firmly together with ribbon or string. I couldn't wait to see if it actually worked!

CHAPTER 5

PREPARATIONS

On Monday at school, everyone was talking about the talent quest. Groups of kids huddled in corners, discussing costumes and props. Everyone seemed to arrive super-early to prepare before class.

Charlie, Meg, Cici and I had arranged to meet in the art room so we could practise. I was on my way to meet them when I walked past the hall. The gym girls were inside wearing their school uniforms and flipping around the stage, cartwheeling in a perfect circle. They all wore gym shorts under their school dresses.

Olivia jumped to her feet. 'It's not *perfect* yet,' she said. 'We need to do it again.'

Sienna pulled an I-can't-believe-it face at Jemila, but the girls obediently took their places to start again.

Olivia glanced over and saw me peeking through the door. She scowled at me for spying and I scurried off.

The other three were already waiting for me in the art room. I dashed in, leaving the door open behind me. This was one of my favourite rooms at school. The room was filled with paint-splattered tables, stools and easels. A collection of clay figures was displayed on a side table. Colourful paintings were hung all over the walls and the shelves were stacked with beautiful art books. Charlie and Cici were perched on a table, strumming their guitars.

'Pippa's here,' said Meg, waving at me.

'Great,' said Cici. 'Let's get started.'

As usual Charlie counted us in, then Charlie and Cici started to play. We all began to sing the lyrics. Meg and I knew all the words to the song now, so we sang loud and strong, with no one to hear us. It was our best run-through yet.

We were so involved that we didn't even notice our teacher, Mrs Marshall, sneak into the room. She stood just inside the door listening to us. When we finished the song, she clapped.

'Well done, girls,' she said. 'That's sounding fabulous. It's great to see you practising so hard.'

I felt a thrill of pleasure at her praise. She was right. It had sounded fabulous.

'We've been rehearsing all weekend,' Cici said.

'It shows,' said Mrs Marshall. 'I can't wait to see you performing it at the audition. Have you worked out your costumes yet?'

'Not yet,' said Charlie. 'That's our plan for today.'

Mrs Marshall's mention of the audition reminded me all over again that tomorrow, we wouldn't be singing this song for fun by ourselves but performing it in front of the whole school. I felt my tummy clench with nerves.

'Good luck with it,' said Mrs Marshall. 'See you in class.'

Mrs Marshall left, leaving us to keep working.

Charlie jiggled up and down, hugging her guitar. 'Mrs Marshall really liked our song. And she's one of the judges!'

Charlie's excitement made my spirits flag.

'But she's right,' said Cici. 'We really do need to decide on our costumes.'

'Maybe we could dress up as animals?' suggested Meg. 'Like cats?'

'No,' said Charlie, shaking her head. 'I think one of the kindy groups has thought of that already.'

'What about a different kind of animal,' suggested Meg. 'Like –'

Meg's favourite animals were dolphins, rhinos and elephants. I imagined standing in front of the whole school dressed up as one of those. The thought made me feel positively ill. Everyone would laugh at us.

'Why can't we just wear our own clothes?' I asked, interrupting her. 'That would be so much easier.' *And we wouldn't look ridiculous*, I thought to myself.

'It's a bit boring though,' said Charlie. 'Half the fun is getting dressed up in something you wouldn't normally wear.'

'A costume would make our act stand out more,' said Cici. 'Especially if it's a little outrageous.'

I could feel a headache coming on. Cici loved wearing quirky and eye-catching fashion. Personally, I preferred to wear clothes that *didn't* stand out.

Meg smiled at me sympathetically. Meg preferred wearing clothes that were comfortable and practical too.

'Perhaps Pippa would feel happier about performing if we wore normal clothes,' suggested Meg. 'Beachy sundresses would suit the song.'

'How about we compromise?' said Charlie. 'We'll wear sundresses to the auditions but if we make it to the concert, we'll come up with something more exciting.'

Cici opened her mouth to object.

'Great idea,' I said quickly, before she could say anything. 'Let's do that.'

Just then the morning bell rang and it was time to start the school day. We went out to join dozens of kids as they emerged from across the playground. We all sat in our class lines, chatting and laughing.

Alex, Rory, Joey and Sam were sitting next to us, whispering madly. I heard words like popping, breaking and locking, which sounded rather violent until I realised they were talking about dance moves. It sounded like the boys were planning on auditioning as well.

It seemed half the school would be up on stage on Tuesday.

Alex turned to me with a smile. 'Are you trying out for the talent quest, Pippa?' he asked. 'Are you going to show us some of your awesome London dance moves?'

I blushed as red as Papa's homegrown tomatoes. All I could think about, of course, was the time I smashed Alex in the nose during dance class. It was not one of my favourite memories and I'd really hoped that Alex had forgotten all about it.

'No,' I mumbled. 'Well, yes we are – but not dancing.'

'What are you doing then?' asked Alex.

Cici leaned over and saved me.

'You'll have to wait and see, Alex,' she said, raising her eyebrows. 'We don't want to spoil the surprise.'

Our day at school was the usual Monday routine of English, maths, reading and art class. The only difference was that at recess and lunch, all anyone seemed to talk about was the audition tomorrow. After school, Charlie and Cici had their regular guitar lessons. I walked to the cafe with Bella and Harry to wait until Mum finished work.

We didn't have any homework, so I took the opportunity to experiment with the fruit crates to see if my bookshelf idea would actually work. There were eight timber crates which I lugged one by one all the way upstairs to my room, then up the ladder. Getting them up the ladder was pretty tricky.

I lay four crates on their side against the round wall to form the bottom layer of my bookshelf. Then I tied them together with brown string to hold them in place. Finally I stacked another three crates on top to form the second layer, which fitted perfectly just under the windows. The last crate was the biggest, so I decided to turn it upside down to make a side table.

There! I'd done it. The tower now had a set of sturdy shelves and a table. My next job was to carefully paint them. I asked Mum if I could use a sample pot of sea-foam-green paint I found in the painting pile. When the crates were painted they looked even better against the white walls.

Next I'd bring some books from the caravan and some pens and pencils. I wondered if Mimi might have an old rug or some cushions we could use to make it cosy. Most of our furniture and knick-knacks were being stored in boxes until the apartment was ready.

Making the shelves was good because it distracted me. But once I'd finished, thoughts of tomorrow's audition crowded in.

Back at the caravan, I packed my bag with my favourite sundress and my sandals. Then I changed my mind and tried another couple of outfits. Nothing seemed right. At last I settled on the first dress again.

All evening there was a heavy feeling in the pit of my stomach, as if I'd accidentally swallowed rocks. I picked at my dinner. For once, bedtime seemed to take forever, and then I couldn't get to sleep for ages. All night, I tossed and turned, having delirious dreams with everyone staring at me frozen on the stage. Would this night ever end?

CHAPTER 6

AUDITIONS

Tuesday morning finally came and I woke up when the alarm went off. I was in the deepest sleep. For a moment I'd forgotten what day it was and then it hit me. Audition day! I felt the familiar heavy lump of dread in my stomach. I burrowed back under the covers and hid my head. Perhaps I could get Mimi to ring the school to say I was too sick to come.

But then I thought about how excited Charlie and Cici were. I couldn't let them down.

I slowly climbed out of bed and grabbed a clean towel.

Harry was already up, standing in his pyjamas at the kitchen table, practising one of his magic tricks.

'Hey, Pippa, watch this,' he said, reaching towards my left ear. He plucked something from my hair. It was a sparkling silver ball with rainbow flashing lights inside it. He tossed the ball up into the air and caught it. Then tossed it and caught it again. But on the third toss he snapped his fingers and it disappeared into thin air.

'Good trick, Harry,' I said, very impressed.

'Thanks,' said Harry. 'It's my new magic ball that Dad sent me. I've been working on it.'

I felt that hollow feeling in the pit of my stomach again. Thinking of Dad always made me feel strange. I pushed the thought firmly away. I had enough to worry about today without thinking of my dad in Switzerland.

I had a shower, ate a couple of mouthfuls of breakfast, then dropped my spoon in my bowl. I really couldn't face eating anything. Mimi stroked my forehead.

'Too nervous to eat, darling?' she said. 'You'll be okay.'

As usual, Mimi and Papa walked us to school.

Bella decided that she wanted to wear her dinosaur costume, even though it was already steaming hot. She carried her tail in one hand so it didn't drag in the dirt. Harry's backpack looked unusually full today. I carried my tote bag with my audition outfit and walked along, leading Summer.

At school there was a definite buzz of excitement in the air. The audition was after lunch. Mrs Marshall tried to keep us working in the morning with our usual maths and English, but everyone was too distracted to focus on lessons. I'd been helping Charlie with her maths, but I had no hope of showing her anything useful today. She was jiggling up and down like corn popping in a hot pan.

When the bell rang at lunchtime we all rushed outside. We were supposed to eat our lunch and then get ready. I was too nervous to eat anything at all.

Kids bustled around carrying musical instruments or wearing their costumes. A group of kindy kids ran past, dressed up as kittens. Olivia, Willow, Sienna, Jemila and Tash were wearing their purple-and-black gym leotards, with their hair brushed into perfect high ponytails. They were warming up outside the hall, doing stretches and knee bends.

Alex, Rory, Sam, Leon, Marcus and Joey were all dressed up with baggy black trousers, white shirts, black vests, white sneakers and back-to-front caps on their heads. They had added oversized, glitzy bling and had bandanas tied around their wrists. They looked nothing like their usual selves.

'Hey,' said Rory, as we walked past. 'What's up, girls?'

He did a little dance with exaggerated hand gestures which made us giggle. The other boys began swaggering and showing off too.

'Hey. Back at you, bro,' said Cici, pretending to be ultra-cool. She's really good at doing funny voices to make us all laugh.

Alex gave us all a quick high five, one after the other.

'Good luck, boys,' said Charlie. 'You look great.'

The four of us went to change out of our uniforms and into our sundresses. When I saw some of the other costumes, I realised most of the kids had gone to a lot of trouble. I suddenly wished that we'd gone with Cici's idea of evening dresses or tutus.

The auditions were being held in the hall. A black velvet curtain had been hung across the back of the stage. Two of the teachers were pinning up a cardboard sign that read 'Kira Cove School Talent Quest'.

A trestle table had been set up for the three judges. There was our year five teacher, Mrs Marshall, and Mr Tzantzaris, the year six teacher. Sitting in the middle was our sometimes crotchety neighbour Mrs Beecham. She was dressed in her best navy suit, with a ruffled white shirt, and was gazing around the room rather critically.

Mrs Beecham had very strong ideas on what she liked and disliked. I knew she hated noisy kids, loud builders, pop music and 'clod-hopping', which was what she called my early attempts at dancing. While Mrs Beecham and I were good friends now, we hadn't started out that way. When the girls and I first met her she had criticised us for being sassy, which in a funny kind of way had inspired the name of our club, the Sassy Sisters.

I wondered what she'd think of our performance. I suddenly felt extra-nervous.

Mrs Beecham was a retired prima ballerina, who had danced in all the major opera houses of the world. I suddenly wished we'd practised a lot more.

I waved to Mrs B, and she waved back regally. Cici was checking the photocopied program.

'Yes! We're going last,' whispered Cici. 'That means we'll be the most memorable.'

Mrs Marshall stood up, holding the microphone. Everyone fell silent.

'Welcome students and teachers to the audition for the Kira Cove School Talent Quest,' she said. Everyone clapped.

'Today is about giving everyone the chance to participate and have fun performing their very own special talents.'

A murmur of excited whispering rippled around the hall.

'We have a special guest here today as one of our judges,' said Mrs Marshall. 'Her name is Mrs Natalya Ivanova Beecham and she was one of the finest ballerinas of her generation. Can you all give Mrs Beecham a huge round of applause.'

It sounded strange to learn Mrs Beecham's full name. A bit like when you find out your teacher's first name. Mrs Beecham suddenly seemed more exotic now that I knew her Russian names.

I settled back to watch the different acts.

The first performance was the cute kindy class. They had dressed up in black leotards with cat ears and tails and drawn whiskers on their faces. They pranced around to a funny song about kitty-cats. Our dance teacher, Miss Demi, stood to the side out the front, doing the actions. Despite this, the kids were all out of time, jumping and pouncing at different moments. One of the boys tripped over his own tail. An adorable girl with both of her front teeth missing had complete stage fright and stood frozen, staring at the judges in terror. I knew exactly how she felt!

The song finished and the twenty little kitty-cats ran off, ears and tails askew. Everyone clapped. The judges scribbled notes.

Next up was a series of kids performing solo. Each one sang pop songs into the microphone, accompanied by a backing track. There were a lot of singers. I began to feel worried. A year three girl played the violin. Oscar played his trumpet solo and Meg's brother, Jack, did a stockwhip-cracking display.

Connor from my class got up to tell some jokes

'Knock knock,' he said.

'Who's there?' roared the crowd.

'A cow.'

'A cow who?' roared the crowd.

'No silly. Cows don't *whooooo*. They *mooooo*.'

The crowd groaned loudly.

'Knock knock,' repeated Connor.

'Who's there?'

'Nanna,' said Connor.

'Nanna who?' came the roared response.

'Nanna your business!'

He bowed and retired to enthusiastic applause. Mr Tzantzaris laughed. I saw Mrs Beecham wince as though she was in pain. I hoped her arthritis wasn't bothering her too much.

The senior band, dressed in their white uniforms, played a rousing jazz piece, which Mrs Beecham clearly loved. She scribbled down more notes in her notebook.

Next up was . . . my sister, Bella, dressed from snout to tail as a ferocious dinosaur. Bella grinned broadly, looking as cute as a cupcake. Then she opened her mouth wide and began to roar as loudly as she could. Bella stomped and chomped and gnashed and clawed as she sang her song.

'Crash. Crash. Stomp your feet.
Gnash. Gnash. Bare your teeth.
Chomp. Chomp. Slash your claws.
Dance the dinosaur romp. ROARRRR!'

I hunched down, wishing the floorboards would open up so I could disappear into a secret tunnel and escape. No such luck! The two minutes of that song felt like an eternity. Mrs Beecham winced again. Her arthritis must definitely be playing up today.

Mrs Marshall nodded encouragingly. 'Thanks so much, Bella. Great costume and your enthusiasm is to be congratulated. Now our next act is the Hip-Hop Boyz . . .'

Bella beamed and bounded off the stage, her tail bouncing behind her.

The stage darkened. Loud rhythmic music began. Boom. Boom. Boom.

The Hip-Hop Boyz swaggered onto the stage, oozing cool confidence. Their dance routine was fast-paced and practised with lots of hops, mock punches and high kicks. The boys finished with a frenetic series of floor spins. They were fantastic.

They sauntered off the stage to the sound

of cheering and clapping. They came and sat in front of us again and I tapped Alex on the shoulder.

'That was brilliant,' I whispered. 'You guys will be chosen for sure.'

Alex smiled back. 'Thanks, Pippa. Good luck for your act. Hope you smash it.'

Luck! We need more than good luck, I thought to myself. *We need a miracle!*

The next act took me completely by surprise. It was my very own brother, Harry. Or more accurately, it was Harry the Marvellous Magician. He wore his black top hat and swirling cape lined with crimson satin. Underneath was a black evening suit, with a white shirt and a crimson bow tie.

'I didn't know Harry was auditioning,' whispered Charlie.

'Neither did I. He didn't mention a word,' I whispered back as Mrs Marshall introduced him.

Harry carried a small black bag which he placed on a table in the centre of the stage. 'Good afternoon, ladies and gentlemen, boys and girls,' said Harry, bowing to the audience. His voice was loud and clear, carrying to the back of the hall. I thought I detected a tiny tell-tale wobble, showing that my brother might be feeling a tad nervous, but it quickly disappeared.

'I am Harry the Marvellous, Master of Magic and Mystery.' Harry swirled his cape, revealing its shiny crimson lining. 'Prepare to be awed and amazed as I reveal to you my magical marvels.'

The audience cheered. Harry took his magic wand and a rectangular purple box from his bag of tricks.

'For my first act, I need to borrow . . . a mobile phone. Would anyone volunteer to give me their phone?'

The audience laughed. No one volunteered.

'Mr Tzantzaris?'

'I don't think so, Harry,' replied Mr Tzantzaris, shaking his head with an amused look on his face.

Harry walked over to him and held out his hand.

'Come on, sir. Don't be frightened. I almost never lose things permanently.'

Mr Tzantzaris reluctantly handed over his phone. Harry held it up for everyone to see.

'Now I am going to make Mr T's phone disappear,' he announced. He opened the purple box, showing the inside to the audience. Then he slipped the phone into the box and waved his magic wand over it.

'Abracadabra. Alakazam!' Harry shouted. He opened the box and tipped it upside down. The mobile phone had disappeared.

Everyone cheered and clapped.

'Where's it gone?' demanded Mr Tzantzaris, pretending to be horrified. 'I need my phone back!'

Harry made a great show of looking in the box. He waved his wand over the box and opened the lid, but it was still empty.

'Mmmm,' he said. 'Let's try that again.'

This time, the phone magically reappeared inside the box and Harry handed it back to its rightful owner. Everyone cheered, Mr Tzantzaris loudest of all.

The next trick involved a blue chiffon scarf. Harry waved it around to show that it was an ordinary square scarf.

'Now I am going to place the scarf inside my magical hand,' explained Harry, as he carefully stuffed the scarf into his closed fist.

Harry tapped the back of his hand three times with his wand, then opened his fist. His hand was empty. There was a collective *'ooh'* from the students.

'It's gone,' cried Harry. 'Now wherever could it be?'

He searched his pockets, then he stepped

down from the stage and walked over to the judges' table.

'Mrs Beecham, I think *you* might have it!'

I giggled at the horrified look on Mrs Beecham's face.

'No, I don't think so,' she insisted. Her Russian accent sounded stronger than usual.

Harry reached behind Mrs Beecham's neck and whipped the scarf from her collar.

'It's *magic*,' he cried. Mrs Beecham shrieked with surprise. Harry strode back to the stage, his cape sweeping behind him.

'And now, for my last and final trick . . .' said Harry. He took off his black top hat and waved it around over his head. 'The greatest magical feat of all.'

The audience craned forward as Harry paused, leaving them all in suspense.

Harry placed his hat upside down on the table. He took his wand and tapped the hat three times.

'Alakazam. Bobbity boo!'

He put his hand inside the hat . . . and pulled out a fluffy, white toy bunny!

The crowd roared with appreciation. Harry bowed left then right and then to the judges' table. Mrs Beecham, Mr Tzantzaris and Mrs Marshall were clapping like mad.

I beamed with pride. Harry's magic performance had been a mega-hit. My brother had done a simply *stupendous* job!

CHAPTER 7

KIRA DREAMING DISASTER

The audition was nearly at an end. There were only two more acts to go.

'And now we have the Fabulous Five,' announced Mr Tzantzaris.

'We're up next,' whispered Cici. 'We need to make sure our act is totally unforgettable.'

Unforgettably brilliant or unforgettably awful? I thought to myself. I had a terrible feeling it might be the latter.

Olivia, Willow, Sienna, Jemila and Tash

leapt gracefully to their feet and walked up the steps onto the stage. They looked very professional in their matching leotards. The music started, blaring out through the hall. The five girls began their gymnastics routine: dancing, walking on their hands and leaping around the stage.

I looked at Charlie, Cici and Meg in absolute horror. The music that was playing on the stage was 'Kira Dreaming', the very same song that we were going to sing in the next act. What a terrible coincidence!

'What are we going to do?' I whispered to the girls. 'We can't sing the exact same song straight after them?'

'We have to,' said Charlie, looking pale. 'We can't change it now.'

Olivia, Jemila, Sienna and Willow froze as Tash did a spectacular solo across the centre of the stage, tumbling and backflipping. The audience roared with appreciation.

All the girls slid into perfectly timed splits. They jumped to their feet and rolled into their whirling circle of successive cartwheels. I could see members of the audience jigging along to the music.

I was watching the girls spinning around when I saw one of them wobble as she neared the edge of the stage. She tried to right herself and then cartwheeled right off the edge. The girl screamed as she fell. I couldn't quite see who it was but it sounded like Tash. The other four girls stopped cartwheeling and rushed over to her.

Mrs Marshall leapt to her feet and dashed over to where the girl lay sprawled on the floor, sobbing. Another teacher rushed to her aid. Someone ran to the office to fetch the school nurse. All the kids were craning their heads to see, whispering about the accident. Mrs Beecham hobbled over with her walking stick to see if she could help.

Mr Tzantzaris turned off the music player and took the microphone.

'Attention please, students,' he said. 'Can we all be patient and quiet while we check that Tash is all right? Nurse Nguyen will be here in just a moment.'

The students quietened down for a moment and then the babble gradually rose again. The school nurse huffed in, carrying her medical kit and an icepack.

From where we were sitting, we could see Nurse Nguyen checking Tash carefully.

'I hope she'll be all right,' I whispered to Charlie.

'That must have hurt a lot,' she replied.

Fortunately, it seemed that Tash hadn't injured herself too badly. Mrs Marshall and Nurse Nguyen helped Tash to a nearby chair where she sat with an icepack on her knee. Olivia, Sienna, Tash and Jemila crowded around her for a moment until Mrs Marshall sent them to sit down.

The nurse had a whispered consultation with the three judges. Mr Tzantzaris took the microphone and stood on the stage. Everyone quietened down again.

'Nurse Nguyen says that Tash will be fine.' There was an outburst of cheering and clapping.

I gave a huge sigh of relief. I really liked Tash and hated to think she might have been seriously hurt.

'But Tash will need to go to the hospital for an X-ray to make sure she hasn't broken anything. In the meantime, we will push on with our audition. We have one more act to watch . . .'

My heart sank. I realised that I was secretly hoping that the rest of the audition would be cancelled.

'Can we please welcome to the stage . . .' Mr Tzantzaris glanced down at his run sheet. 'The Sassy Sisters!'

Charlie, Cici and Meg jumped to their feet.

Charlie leaned down and grabbed my hand, her eyes shining with excitement. 'Come on, Pippa.'

I walked reluctantly towards the stage, following my friends. My sundress felt all sweaty, sticking to the back of my legs. My mouth was so dry it felt like it was stuffed with Kira Beach sand. I took a shaky breath as we climbed the steps onto the stage.

Meg and I fetched two high stools that were waiting for us behind the curtains and lugged them onto the stage. Cici and Charlie sat on the stools and tuned their guitars. Meg and I stood on either side of them, holding the microphones.

Cici took the microphone from Meg. 'Good morning, ladies and gentlemen. We are the Sassy Sisters, and this is one of our favourite songs – "Kira Dreaming".'

There was a round of applause.

Charlie and Cici began to play the opening chords. I took another raspy breath and licked my lips. My heart was hammering so loudly I thought everyone in the hall must be able to hear it. I glanced towards the judges' table. Mrs Beecham gave me an encouraging smile. I grimaced back.

And then – I dropped the microphone. It just slipped out of my sweaty hand. The mic hit the stage with a loud clang. The noise was amplified throughout the hall, followed by a ripple of laughter. My whole body went scorching hot with embarrassment and I scrambled down on all fours to pick it up. Charlie looked at me in absolute horror. The girls stopped playing.

'Sorry,' I mumbled, glancing at the others in panic. I *knew* this was a terrible idea. Why on earth had I let the girls talk me into this?

Meg flashed me a reassuring smile. I heard Charlie start the countdown again. 'One, two, three . . .' Her voice sounded wobbly. Cici and Charlie began playing the opening chords, then the three of them began to sing. I just kind of opened my mouth and pretended. I thought the girls would do a better job without me.

Their singing wasn't bad. But it wasn't that great either. I'd heard them sing much better when we were painting.

After all the polished performances by the other kids and the excitement of Tash's accident, our song fell rather flat. The girls seemed to hurry through it to get it done as quickly as possible. It wasn't helped by the fact that part way through our song Mrs Nguyen helped Tash out of the hall. Everybody craned their necks and whispered madly as they watched her hobble out. Mr Tzantzaris had to stand up and glare at everyone to get them to settle down.

It was with great relief that we sang the last note. The audience clapped politely and we scurried off the stage.

'Well, we did it,' said Meg encouragingly.

I just felt happy that it was finally over.

'Not brilliantly,' said Cici, looking really disappointed. 'I'm glad Ruby didn't hear that effort.'

'There's no way we'll be invited to sing at the concert after that,' said Charlie. She looked like she was fighting back tears. 'It was terrible.'

'I'm sorry,' I said, feeling a wave of guilt. 'I didn't mean to drop the mic. I just felt so nervous.'

Charlie didn't look at me. She stared really intently at the curtains.

Meg squeezed my arm. 'It was an accident. You couldn't help it.'

We took our seats. Olivia shot a glance at me. I couldn't tell if it was a look of sympathy or if she was secretly enjoying my embarrassment.

Mrs Beecham, Mr Tzantzaris and Mrs Marshall were conferring, reading their notes and discussing their thoughts on which acts should be performed at the VIP concert.

It seemed the three couldn't agree. The discussion looked quite heated as Mrs Beecham stubbornly shook her head. Mrs Marshall glanced over towards where we were seated in the audience, then whispered madly. Mr Tzantzaris threw his arms in the air. At last Mrs Beecham nodded her head.

She stood up, leaning on her stick, and hobbled onto the stage. She seemed to grow taller as she stood there and took the microphone.

'Girls and boys of Kira Cove Primary School,' said Mrs Beecham. 'It has been such an honour to be one of the judges at your talent quest. There was such a broad range of performances showcased today, from singing to gymnastics, to magic and my greatest love – dance! It has been a difficult decision to choose only five acts to perform on Friday.'

Mrs Beecham looked around the hall.

'But after much discussion, the winning acts

are: The Kindy Kitty-cats, the Kira Cove Senior Band, the Hip-Hop Boyz, Harry the Marvellous Magician ... And finally, the Fabulous Five gymnastics troupe.'

There was a roar of approval from the students as each act was announced. The Kindy Kitty-cats wriggled with excitement. The Hip-Hop Boyz high-fived each other. Only the four remaining gymnasts from the Fabulous Five were looking gloomy, despite their win.

Charlie slumped beside me, her whole body drooping with disappointment.

'Never mind,' I said to her.

'I know *you* don't care,' said Charlie, her voice shaking with emotion. 'You made it quite clear you didn't want to do it, and you didn't even *try* to sing up there.'

'I ... I ...' I began. But I didn't know what to say. Charlie was obviously very upset with me.

Charlie turned away and sniffed. Meg gave her a hug. Charlie shrugged it off and wriggled away.

Mrs Marshall took the microphone and called for attention.

'Thanks so much to all the students who auditioned,' she said. 'I can see that a lot of effort went into planning acts, preparing costumes and rehearsing. It takes a lot of courage to get up in front of the whole school and perform – and you all did a marvellous job.'

Everyone cheered and clapped, except the Sassy Sisters. We were too disheartened.

'Now we're going to have an early mark today, so let's all go back to our classrooms to pack up,' said Mrs Marshall. There was more applause as the kids realised that they could go home early. Everyone jumped to their feet and crowded out of the hall. I climbed to my feet more slowly, feeling upset and confused.

As I stood up I felt really light-headed.

I suddenly realised I'd hardly eaten anything since yesterday. I closed my eyes to steady myself.

Charlie raced off and I tried to catch up with her to talk, but I couldn't fight my way through the throngs. I was separated from Meg and Cici too.

Outside in the playground I looked around but the girls had disappeared. My heart sank. Were all three girls furious with me for mucking up our act? Would they ever talk to me again?

Alex bounded up to me in his hip-hop outfit of baggy black pants and a back-to-front cap. He did a little dance skip, waving his arms back and forth and jerking his head.

'Hey, Pippa,' he said in a funny voice. 'Where's your mic?'

He pretended to throw me something, then mimed fumbling it and turned it into an exaggerated dance move. He looked like a crazy, black-and-white robot.

'What are you doing, Alex?' I asked sharply.

Alex stopped dancing.

'You know,' he said, grinning at me. 'Dropping the mic on stage. That was pretty funny.'

I glared at him, my face burning with shame. 'It wasn't funny at all, Alex.'

I spun on my heel and stormed off.

'Pippa,' Alex called after me. 'I was only joking.'

Alex's 'joke' really stung. I wondered if everyone was laughing at me. It made me feel even worse.

By the time I arrived in the classroom, everyone had gone.

When I'd packed my backpack, I went to meet my brother and sister to walk them back to the cafe. For once I had no trouble dragging Bella out of the playground. She was sitting quietly on a seat by herself. Her dinosaur suit was in a bag beside her. I was glad to see that she'd finally changed out of it. Harry came up to join us.

While I felt totally humiliated every time I thought about my own performance, I was super-proud of Harry's success.

'Congratulations, Harry,' I said, giving my brother a high five. 'You did a brilliant job with your magic show. You really deserved to be one of the winners.'

Bella gave a loud sniff.

'Thanks, Pippa,' said Harry. 'I'm pretty happy.'

'You didn't look nervous at all,' I said, feeling envious. 'You were really professional. Unlike me. I felt ill up there.'

Harry grinned back at me, his dark hair standing on end. He paused as though thinking whether to say more.

'Yeah. Dad told me a secret trick,' Harry blurted out. 'He said you look out at the audience and imagine that everyone is sitting there in their underwear. Then you don't feel so scared.'

I couldn't help but smile at the idea of a whole audience without clothes. But the mention of Dad threw me. 'Really? When did Dad tell you that?'

Harry looked a bit uncomfortable. 'On Saturday, when you and Mum were at the cafe. He rang on Mimi and Papa's phone and I told him about my tricks. But don't tell Mum. I don't want her to be sad that I talked to Dad.'

'Mum wouldn't be sad . . .' I began to object. But Harry and I both knew that everyone in the family acted a bit weird and awkward whenever Dad called. Last time he rang, I couldn't think of anything to say at all and Bella had cried for an hour afterwards.

'Okay,' I promised.

'You too, Bella,' said Harry. 'Don't tell Mum.'

Bella gave a strangled sob. She dragged her dinosaur onesie out of its bag and hugged its green furry head tightly to her chest.

'Are you all right, Bella?' I asked suspiciously. I'd never once had Bella waiting quietly for me. And come to think of it, her eyes were all red and puffy as though she'd been crying.

Bella sniffed again.

'I . . . I . . . wanted to do my dinosaur song at the special performance because *Dad* would come to see it,' said Bella. 'He always came to our end of year concerts in London.'

Then Bella burst into loud, noisy sobs. I didn't know what to do. There was no way Dad would be coming all the way from Switzerland to see a talent quest on tiny Kira Island. Bella wiped her eyes on the dinosaur head. I sat down next to her and gave her a hug.

'It's okay, Bella-boo.' I said soothingly. 'Not everyone can perform. Charlie's really sad that we didn't make it through too. But maybe we just didn't have the right acts this time?'

Bella nodded and hiccupped.

'Come on,' I said. 'Let's go back to the cafe

and I'll make you a Mango Madness smoothie for a special treat.'

Bella jumped up, carrying her dinosaur suit in her arms like a teddy bear. She smeared away the tears streaking her face.

Bella's disappointment reminded me of Charlie's reaction. I had the terrible feeling that it was my fault we hadn't done a better job. The other girls had tried really hard, but I'd been against the idea from the start. I realised I hadn't tried my best at all. I was too busy worrying about what everyone would think. Now I'd let my closest friends down. The thought made me feel sick with shame. Whatever could I do to fix this mess?

CHAPTER 8

THE MANGO MADNESS BURGLAR

Back at the cafe, Harry and I tried our best to cheer up Bella. Mum was upstairs checking on the builders and Zoe was busy making drinks for a big group of businesspeople who were having a meeting out on the jetty. We sat Bella down at my favourite table in the corner by the window seat.

Harry and I made Bella's special Mango Madness smoothie. This smoothie is an amazing blend of mango, pineapple and frozen banana with creamy yoghurt, milk and loads of ice. Harry and I invented it when we were experimenting one day.

I even brought her a dinosaur cupcake to cheer her up. These were the latest addition to the cupcake menu. Mini vanilla cupcakes with whipped vanilla cream and a green jelly dinosaur perched on top. Cici had created them especially for Bella because she was so besotted with dinosaurs.

Bella picked the dinosaur off the top and nibbled at that. She took a few sips of her smoothie then pushed it aside.

Harry tried to coax a smile out of Bella by making his silver ball appear from behind her ear and then disappear into thin air. Bella just sniffed back a sob. It looked like our plan to cheer Bella up with Mango Madness had been a complete failure.

Then, as I was rinsing the blender in the kitchen, I saw Harry whispering something in her ear. Bella grinned up at him. She took a quick gulp of her smoothie and then the two of them disappeared upstairs to our empty apartment. I wondered what on earth they could be up to.

Bella had left her smoothie cup and her cupcake on the table. I put the milk and yoghurt back in the fridge. Suddenly, I heard a terrible crash and spun around. Out of the corner of my eye I saw a dark shadow dart under the tables.

I soon realised the cause of the crash. Someone or something had knocked over Bella's smoothie cup. Maybe it was a gust of wind? Mango, banana and pineapple smoothie had pooled all over the table.

'*Bella!*' I cried. There was no answer.

Why couldn't she clean up after herself? Now I'd have to do it.

I grabbed a cloth to clean up yet another mess. It was then I noticed that there were funny little mango smudges all over the table. I took a closer look. They weren't smudges. They were tiny paw prints. It looked like some kind of animal had knocked over Bella's smoothie while trying to drink it. But what? I quickly mopped up the mess, my mind ticking over different explanations.

There was a mystery behind those paw prints and I was going to solve it. I was just about to head upstairs to recruit Harry and Bella to help me with the search, when the cafe phone rang.

Mum was still upstairs and Zoe was carrying a heavy tray of drinks outside. Mum had taught us how to answer the cafe phone if we needed to.

'Hello? The Beach Shack Cafe,' I said in my most professional voice. 'Pippa speaking. Can I help you?'

There was a silent pause. 'Hello?' I said again.

'Pippa, sweetheart. Is that you?' came a terribly familiar voice. My heart lurched. It was my dad. He sounded like he could be standing right beside me in the kitchen. I blinked back sudden hot tears.

'Are you there, Pippa? It's me, Dad – calling from Switzerland.'

A tumult of emotions welled up inside me. Joy at hearing his voice again. Sorrow at missing him. Anger at him for leaving us. Confusion at how I felt about Mum. Was I being disloyal to her by talking to Dad when he had hurt us all so badly?

'Pippa? Talk to me, please?' begged Dad. 'How are you?'

'Fine,' I said with gritted teeth. But I wasn't fine at all.

I thought about my family and how hard it had been since Dad left us – losing our home, moving to the other side of the world, starting a new life, having no money, working so hard to start the cafe. I thought about Bella crying because Dad wouldn't be there to see her perform her dino romp. I thought about Harry practising and practising his magic tricks because it reminded him of Dad and the fun times they'd shared together. I thought of Mum and how tired and sad she looked sometimes when she thought no one was looking.

'How's everything going?' asked Dad. 'How's Bella? How's Harry? How's Mum?'

It was anger that won. I wanted to shout and scream and cry at Dad and ask him why he'd left. All my frustration at this terrible day overcame me.

'How do you think we're going?' I blurted out. 'It's been terrible. Harry doesn't say anything but he misses you so much. Bella's upset because she thought you'd come to our school concert. And Mum's working day and night to make the cafe a success and as hard as she tries to be cheerful, I know she's really, really sad sometimes. '

I could hear Dad take in a sharp breath.

'I'm sorry, Pippa,' said Dad. 'I know it's been difficult. I miss you all so much.'

'If you missed us, you'd be here with us,' I cried. 'I don't understand why you left.'

'I know you're angry and upset,' said Dad. 'And that's okay. It will take a little while to get used to everything being different.'

I didn't say anything – I was just trying my hardest not to cry. I glanced around the cafe to see if anyone had noticed my outburst.

'I've moved into a nice little apartment in the centre of Geneva,' gabbled Dad, sounding desperate. 'It's just a short walk from work. It has lovely views of the lake and the mountains. I was hoping you three kids could come and stay with me in the holidays. Maybe we could go skiing in January.'

'Dad, I can't really talk now,' I said quietly. I didn't want to go to Switzerland. I didn't want to see Dad's new life that he'd made without us.

'I've tried ringing a few times but there's been no answer on your mum's phone,' said Dad. 'I even rang your grandparents' home phone last weekend and spoke to Harry.'

I thought of the couple of times Mum's phone had rung and she hadn't taken the call. I remembered Mum had looked upset. It must have been Dad ringing.

'We've been kind of busy,' I said awkwardly. Mum's voice came from above, talking to the builders. I could hear the four of them clumping down the stairs. I didn't want Mum to find me talking to Dad in case it upset her. 'Sorry, Dad. I have to go.'

I hung up and scurried off. Dad's call seemed to be the final straw in a day that had gone from bad to worse. My bad mood reminded me of how upset Bella had been this afternoon, so I thought I'd better check on her.

Bella and Harry were upstairs in the partly finished living room of the apartment. Harry had hung up an old tablecloth between two stepladders to create a makeshift curtain. Bella was hiding behind it. Harry pulled back the curtain and Bella jumped out, roaring and snarling, her fingers clenched into claws.

'Tada!' cried Harry. 'And here she is, magically reappeared.'

Bella took a bow.

'Are you all right, Bella?' I asked.

'Yes, of course,' replied Bella, looking at me as though I was crazy.

'I wondered if you were still feeling sad?' I asked. 'About not performing in the concert?'

Bella beamed at me

'But I *am* performing in the concert,' she announced. 'I'm going to be Harry the Marvellous Magician's assistant and chief victim.'

'Victim?' I asked in astonishment.

'Harry's going to make me magically disappear,' said Bella.

'What do you mean?' I cried, staring at Harry. 'You can't be serious?'

127

'He says he can bring me back, just like the mobile phone,' insisted Bella.

Harry laughed. 'I'm not really going to make her disappear. I'm just going to create the *illusion* of Bella disappearing. Papa is helping me build a magic box that's big enough for a person.'

I couldn't possibly imagine how Harry could create the illusion of Bella disappearing on stage. But that was the beauty of Harry's magic tricks. I didn't know how he did any of them.

'That sounds brilliant,' I said. 'But why didn't you do the act today?'

'We haven't finished making the box yet,' said Harry. 'It took longer than I thought and I need to test that it works. But Papa and I should finish it tonight. Then Bella and I can try doing it properly.'

'And I get to wear a really cool costume,' said Bella. She was skipping with excitement.

'Let me guess? A dinosaur?' I asked. 'Or a magician?'

'No, silly. A tiger,' replied Bella.

I looked at Harry with admiration. Half an hour ago Bella was miserable and now she was delirious with happiness.

'That's a fantastic idea,' I said. 'I can't wait to see you perform this trick!'

'Wouldn't Dad love to see us?' said Bella. 'I bet he'll come and surprise us at the concert.'

Harry and I exchanged a wordless glance. Well, there's no way that would be happening.

I suddenly thought of an idea to distract Bella from talk of Dad.

'You know, I think I've solved the mystery of the disappearing cafe food,' I said.

'Is it magic?' asked Bella, with round eyes. 'Like Harry does?'

'What disappearing cafe food?' asked Harry.

'For the last few days food has been disappearing from the cafe,' I explained. 'First it was Zoe's ham sandwich, then Bella's toastie and just now something knocked over Bella's smoothie.'

129

Bella pouted. 'I hadn't finished with that.'

'Well, whoever knocked over your smoothie left tiny mango paw prints,' I said.

'Could it be a rat?' asked Harry.

I shook my head. 'The paws were too big for a rat. But why don't we go and see if we can find it?'

The three of us clattered down the stairs to the cafe, keen to begin our search for the food burglar. Much to my astonishment, there was someone waiting for me by the counter. Zoe raised an eyebrow at me and smiled. 'You have a visitor.'

It was Alex. He had changed out of his hip-hop outfit and was wearing an everyday T-shirt and board shorts.

'Hi, Pippa,' he said, looking very sheepish. 'Um . . .'

I wasn't in the mood for Alex and his not-so-funny jokes. Zoe hustled Harry and Bella away to help her clear some messy tables.

'Yes?' I asked, putting on my best polite, for-customers voice. 'Can I get you something?'

'No, um, thanks,' said Alex. 'Actually, I brought you something.'

He pulled a big block of milk chocolate from his backpack. 'It's for you . . . I just wanted to say sorry for upsetting you today. I didn't mean to make fun of you dropping the microphone. I was just trying to make you laugh.'

I looked at the block of chocolate in absolute astonishment. Alex was here with a present for me, to say sorry for upsetting me.

'Pippa?' asked Alex. 'Are you all right? I really am sorry.'

Alex's apology suddenly made me feel a whole lot better. I knew how hard it was to say sorry when you had accidentally hurt some-one's feelings. Alex pushed the chocolate into my hand.

'Thanks, Alex,' I said. 'That's really nice of you.'

'No problem,' he said. 'By the way, I liked the song you guys sang.'

'It was the others,' I admitted. 'I didn't really sing at all. I was too embarrassed about throwing the microphone all over the stage.'

Alex laughed. 'You weren't that bad.'

I shrugged, pulling a face of disbelief. He looked awkward for a moment.

'Anyway, I have to head home now,' he said. 'I just didn't want you to be upset about me being an idiot . . .'

'I'm okay,' I said. 'Thanks.'

He waved as he headed out the front door.

'Bye, Alex,' I called.

What a surprise, I thought to myself. *Who'd have thought that Alex would come and make such a thoughtful apology?* But this wasn't the last mystery of the afternoon. Today was turning out to be full of surprises.

CHAPTER 9

CAPTURING THE CULPRIT

'We've just been robbed again,' said Zoe, as I walked over to join them. 'That poltergeist is back to its old tricks.'

'What's happened?' I asked, looking around.

'We were clearing this table and I noticed that the customer had left a scrap of sliced cheese on their plate,' said Zoe. 'I turned around to load Harry up with plates and when I turned back, the scrap of cheese had disappeared, right off the plate.'

'What's a polta guy?' asked Bella.

'A *poltergeist*,' said Zoe. 'It's a naughty spirit or ghost that causes mayhem by making loud noises or throwing things around. Or in this case stealing food.'

Bella looked worried.

'It's not really a ghost,' I said. 'I think it's some sort of animal.' I told Zoe about the smudgy paw prints in Bella's spilt smoothie.

'Let's see if we can track it down,' said Harry. 'There must be some clues somewhere.'

'Well, let me know when you find the thief,' said Zoe. 'I have some harsh words to say to whoever or whatever has been stealing our food.'

So Harry, Bella and I crept around the cafe looking for clues to find the mysterious cafe thief. We searched between the tables, looking for something that might have been dropped – some crust, some abandoned scraps or some paw prints. We checked the tables to see if anything else had been knocked over and smashed. We went out the back onto the jetty overlooking the cove to see if there was a strange animal lurking in the shadows.

We didn't find anything.

We went out the front of the cafe but all there was to be found was the old rowboat filled with pots of lush herbs and vegetables. The gnarled frangipani, hung with silver lanterns, swayed and jingled in the breeze.

'What's that?' asked Bella. 'I heard something.'

'It was just the lanterns swinging in the tree,' I said.

'No,' said Bella, poking behind the rowboat. 'I heard a little cry.'

'I heard it too,' said Harry with excitement. 'It came from under the jetty.'

The three of us crawled down onto the sand that led under the Beach Shack. The water lapped up under most of the boatshed, but above the high-tide mark was the soft, sandy beach. Right up where our jetty met the esplanade was a low, dark cave.

We heard the soft cry again. Some debris had washed into the cave during a storm and formed a nest made of cardboard and plastic. Huddled in the middle of the nest was a tiny black-and-white kitten with big green eyes.

The kitten spat and hissed at us, its fur standing up on end.

'She's frightened,' I whispered. 'I wonder if her mother's nearby.'

'Can we take her home?' asked Bella.

'It depends if she belongs to someone,' Harry said.

'She wouldn't be living under our jetty if she belonged to someone,' I replied. 'She must be lost.'

'She looks hungry,' said Bella.

The little kitten did look thin and scrawny. I guessed that she wouldn't have been stealing scraps from the cafe if she had a mother looking after her.

'Here kitty, kitty, kitty . . .' I called, holding

out my fingers. The kitten retreated further under the jetty, hissing at us.

'Harry, go and get some food for her,' I said. 'Some cheese or meat, and bring a box and a towel . . . I'll stay here and make sure she doesn't run away.'

Harry looked like he was going to argue, but then he wriggled out backwards. A moment later I could hear his footsteps thundering overhead as he raced inside the cafe.

In a few minutes he crawled back with a cardboard box, a folded towel and a container of shredded chicken.

'I asked Zoe and she said to try the chicken,' said Harry, nearly bumping his head on the jetty above.

I lay on my stomach and held out a piece of chicken meat, holding my breath.

'Stay really still,' I warned. 'Bella, don't make a sound.'

Miraculously my little sister lay still, watching

the kitten. I don't think I've ever seen her be so quiet for so long.

Nothing happened.

I decided it might help if I made soft little meow noises like Trixie.

'Meow. Meow,' I crooned.

'Mew,' the kitten replied.

'Meow. Meow,' I crooned again.

The kitten inched forward, its little pink nose twitching. I held the shred of chicken out temptingly. At last the kitten couldn't resist and dashed forward to snatch the morsel from my fingers. The kitten retreated to its nest and gobbled the meat. I held out another shred.

She came more quickly this time. After feeding her several scraps, I caught hold of the kitten. She struggled and hissed, trying to scratch me. Harry passed me the towel, and I quickly wrapped her up and popped her inside the cardboard box.

We crawled out and took her up to the cafe.

Mum and Zoe were in the kitchen.

'Look, we found the cafe thief,' I said. 'Or should I say, we've found the kitty-cat burglar!' We all crowded around the box.

'She's *soooo* cute,' said Bella.

Mum opened the lid of the box and peeked in. The kitten had escaped from the towel and looked up at us with big green eyes. She mewed pitifully.

'So this is the little waif who's been stealing our food,' said Zoe, with a laugh. 'She is utterly divine.'

'Such a little scrap of a thing,' said Mum. 'Where did you find her?'

We told Mum the story about the stolen cheese and searching for the culprit.

'She looks like she's either lost or abandoned,' said Mum. 'We'd better take her to see the vet.'

'Can't we keep her, Mum?' pleaded Bella.

'Yes. Yes. *Pleeease*,' begged Harry.

Mum gazed at the three of us as we jiggled up

and down with excitement. Then she looked at the kitten with its huge, frightened green eyes.

'She may have an owner who is terribly sad that she's lost,' said Mum.

'But we rescued her,' I said. 'She might have died if we hadn't found her. Look how skinny she is.'

'Let me ring Caitlin and we'll see what she says,' said Mum.

Mum rang the vet hospital and Caitlin told us to bring the kitten down straight away. Of course Harry, Bella and I all insisted on coming along, so Mum left Zoe to finish closing up while we were gone.

Willow was sitting at the front desk in the waiting room when we arrived. Willow took a quick peek at the kitten cowering in the cardboard box in Mum's arms. Then she showed us in to see her mum in the consulting room.

Caitlin took the little kitten out of the box and examined her. The kitten hissed and spat.

'Her little heart is beating so fast,' said Caitlin, gently stroking the kitten's head. 'She's frightened of us.'

Caitlin worked quickly and efficiently to treat the kitten without scaring her too much. She weighed her and listened to her heartbeat with a stethoscope. Mum made sure we stood well back so we didn't crowd the tiny patient.

'Judging from her size, she's about seven weeks old, but very underweight, so our first job is to feed her up,' said Caitlin. 'It's lucky you found her when you did. She's half-starved.'

I felt a wave of sorrow for our little kitten – left hungry and all alone.

Caitlin scanned the kitten to see if she had been microchipped but there was nothing there. 'How long do you think she's been stealing scraps from the cafe?' she asked.

'Since at least Friday,' I said. 'That's when she stole Zoe's sandwich.'

'We haven't had anyone call us to report a missing kitten,' said Caitlin. 'So I'd say she's been abandoned.'

'Who would abandon a tiny kitten?' I asked, feeling horrified.

'You'd be surprised, Pippa, how thoughtless people can be,' said Caitlin. 'Some people just can't be bothered to look after their animals properly. In any case, I think we can safely assume this little one doesn't have an owner.'

Caitlin explained that she would put up a notice in the vet hospital in case anyone had lost her.

'So now we need to decide what to do with her,' said Caitlin. 'The kitten needs to be kept in a warm, secure crate for a couple of days and fed frequently until she gets used to having people around. Then she needs to be socialised with lots of cuddling, snuggling and playing every day so she becomes a gorgeous pet instead of a wild feral cat.'

I imagined snuggling and cuddling with our very own pet kitten. I couldn't think of anything better.

Caitlin looked at Mum, then at each of us. 'I could keep her here at the vet hospital and try to find a good home for her,' she offered.

'Can't we look after her, Mum?' I begged. 'Please. She would have died if we hadn't saved her.'

'We can pay for her food and medicine,' said Harry. 'You can have all my pocket money.'

'And mine too,' said Bella. '*Please*, Mum?'

The kitten mewed, making Mum burst out laughing. 'What chance do I have when all four of you are looking at me with those big hopeful eyes? All right, we can take her home.'

Harry, Bella and I jumped up and down, squealing with delight, until the kitten hissed and reminded us that she wasn't used to humans, especially noisy kids.

Caitlin explained everything that we needed to do. She loaded us up with a secure kitten crate, bedding, water and food bowls, special kitten food and lots of instructions.

'Try to keep her crate somewhere up high so she can hear and see everything that's going on,' said Caitlin. 'And then she's safe from your mischievous Summer as well.'

'We need to think of a really special name for her,' I said.

'Blackie,' said Bella. 'Or Shadow.'

Too obvious, I thought.

'Morgana,' said Harry. 'Or Guinevere.'

Too fancy, I thought.

'How about Winter?' said Mum. 'Then we'd have sunny Summer and stormy Winter?'

None of those names seemed to suit our super-cute, tiny scrap of a cat. I thought back to the clues that had helped us find her. The smudges of mango paw prints and the sneaky way she stole food.

'How about Smudge?' I said. And somehow Smudge was the name that stuck.

Back home in the caravan, we fed Smudge some tinned kitten food from a spoon. Caitlin said we shouldn't handle her much for the first two days, which was torture. All of us wanted to cuddle her and make a fuss of her. But Mum was firm. If any of us broke the rules, Smudge would have to go back to the vet hospital. We made her a comfortable nest and set her kitten crate up on top of the dining table so Summer couldn't reach her.

I crawled into bed, my head buzzing with everything that had happened. It had been the worst day, and yet the best day. The audition had been a disaster, but finding Smudge had been a wonderful adventure. I couldn't wait to tell Charlie and Cici and Meg at school tomorrow. But that reminded me that Charlie was still cross with me about the audition. Maybe the news of our stray kitten Smudge would win her over?

CHAPTER 10

TUTU TIME

In the morning I fed Smudge her breakfast from a spoon. Caitlin had said that feeding her from a spoon would encourage her to associate good things (yummy food) with kind humans (us). It also meant she couldn't gobble down her food too fast. We weren't allowed to feed her with our fingers because that might encourage her to bite us (ouch!).

It seemed to be working because Smudge didn't seem quite so quaky.

Summer was absolutely fascinated by our new visitor. While I fed Smudge, Summer sat on my foot with her tongue hanging out, begging for a taste. Summer had obviously decided that Smudge's breakfast looked far more delicious than her own.

'I'll take Smudge to work with me so I can feed her during the day,' said Mum, packing up a bag of kitten food and bowls. 'She can stay in the crate at the cafe. That will help her get used to people and noise.'

'I can take the day off school to look after her,' I said helpfully. 'Mimi and Papa will be here.' I would have loved to stay home to look after Smudge, but the truth was I was nervous about seeing Charlie, Cici and Meg at school in case they were still upset with me. And I was worried that the other kids would still be laughing at my microphone juggling skills. Staying home with Smudge was definitely a better idea.

'No way, young lady,' said Mum with a laugh. 'Mimi and Papa have enough to do looking after Summer without adding a crotchety cat to the mix. And you need to go to school.'

'Nice try,' Harry said, smirking at me over his breakfast bowl. I pulled a face back at him and closed the door of the crate.

For today and tomorrow, Smudge would stay snug in her crate with lots of little meals to fatten her up. We could gradually start snuggling her on Thursday and then on Friday she could start exploring.

The distraction of Smudge made us all run late, so Mimi drove us to school for a change. In the playground I found the others near the big tree. It was already hot and steamy. I could feel a trickle of sweat running down my back.

Cici and Meg called hello. I answered a bit awkwardly.

'Are you feeling all right, Pippa?' asked Meg, looking at me with concern.

'I'm fine,' I said.

Charlie looked away. It seemed she was still upset with me about not trying yesterday.

I thought about Alex and his unexpected apology and how it made me feel better.

'Sorry about mucking up the audition yesterday,' I said, feeling ashamed. 'I was just so nervous. And when I dropped the microphone I felt like such an idiot . . .'

'That's okay,' said Meg. 'You couldn't help it.'

Meg's kindness made me feel a little better.

'I didn't sing up there and I should have at least tried,' I admitted. 'I thought I'd just make everything worse. But now I feel terrible, because I know how much it meant to all of you.'

'It was bad luck going after Tash's accident,' said Cici. 'That threw all of us off. None of us sang as well as we could have.'

Charlie thought for a moment, playing with the end of her plait. She shrugged, then gave me a crooked half-smile. 'You're right. We were all pretty awful.'

I gave an inward sigh of relief. It looked like I'd been forgiven.

'In other news,' I said, changing the subject, 'we've discovered who the cafe thief is. And she's absolutely adorable.'

'Really?' asked Cici, immediately curious. 'Who was it?'

'A tiny black-and-white kitten. We've called her Smudge,' I replied.

I told the girls the story of apprehending the kitty-cat burglar under the boatshed. They all asked questions and by the time I had finished telling them the story, all the awkwardness had been forgotten.

'So now you have one mum, three rambunctious kids, one mischievous puppy *and* a thieving kitten living in your caravan?' joked Charlie. 'Now that's chaos!'

I grinned broadly. 'At least Bella isn't practising her dino romp anymore.'

Charlie was back to her normal, joking self. What a relief! No one likes falling out with their best friends.

We drifted over to hang with the other year fives under the big tree.

'Do you know how Tash is?' asked Alex.

Olivia, Jemila, Willow and Sienna all looked super-gloomy.

'She won't be coming to school today,' said Jemila.

'I heard she's been flown to a hospital on the mainland,' said Rory.

'Really?' asked Cici. 'That's awful.'

'No, she hasn't,' said Willow. 'The doctor just wants her to stay at home for a couple of days.'

'That's such a shame,' I said. 'Will she be okay?'

Olivia bit her lip. 'The doctor said nothing is broken, which is the good news, but the really bad news is that Tash won't be able to do any gymnastics for at least six weeks. She strained her knee.'

'Oh no,' said Meg. 'Poor Tash.'

Sienna sighed deeply. 'And that means that we can't perform at the concert on Friday.'

'We can't have the Fabulous Five with only four gymnasts,' explained Willow.

'Couldn't you adapt your routine?' I asked. 'Maybe you could be the Fabulous Four?'

Olivia tossed her ponytail in disgust. 'It's obvious you don't do gymnastics. The routine wouldn't work without our star gymnast and we don't have enough time to change it. It takes weeks of rehearsal to get it perfect. We're going to have to pull out.'

I bristled at Olivia's snarky tone, but then I realised that she wasn't trying to be mean to me. She was just upset about Tash. We all were.

At recess, I spotted a rather surprising visitor in the playground. It was Mrs Beecham, hobbling out of the school office. I raced over to say hello.

'Hello, Pippa dear,' said Mrs Beecham, leaning on her stick. 'I'm pleased you saw me. I'd like to talk to you about something.'

Mrs Beecham looked serious, which made me feel rather nervous. Had I done something wrong?

'Did you enjoy the talent quest auditions yesterday?' I asked.

'That's what I want to speak with you about,' she said. 'Mrs Marshall has informed me that the gymnastics troupe can no longer perform on Friday because of Tash's injury.'

'I know,' I said. 'The girls told us this morning.'

Mrs Beecham looked around the playground as kids raced past, screeching and hooting.

'I'm not much of a gymnastics fan,' confessed Mrs Beecham, 'though I really loved the dancing component of their act. But if the girls can't perform, I think that you and your friends should take their place.'

I shook my head, thinking of what a terrible ordeal the audition had been. Mrs Beecham ignored my protest.

'You were the runners-up,' she said. 'Mrs Marshall felt that your performance was significantly disadvantaged by coming after Tash's accident. She told Mr Tzantzaris and I that she saw you all rehearsing a few days ago and you did a marvellous job.'

I felt hot with embarrassment. 'It was me who let the girls down. I had terrible stage fright.'

Mrs Beecham leaned towards me and patted my hand. 'I saw you girls sing at the cafe a couple of weeks ago, and it was lovely,' she said. 'I told the judges I had full faith that you could do a magnificent job for the VIP concert.'

This very rare praise from our crotchety

neighbour was a thrill. However, being Mrs Beecham, there was definitely a 'but' . . .

'Nevertheless, you'd need to do a lot of work by Friday,' she told me sternly. 'The singing would need to be a lot stronger than what we saw yesterday, and you all need to work on your stage presence. It was quite static, so perhaps some choreography and some colourful costumes would help.'

I thought for a moment. Did I want to perform again after the humiliation of making a fool of myself on stage? What if I dropped the microphone a second time? Or fell off the stage like Tash?

Some of my fear must have shown on my face. Mrs Beecham's expression softened.

'You mustn't let negative thoughts crowd your mind, Pippa, or you'll talk yourself into failing,' said Mrs Beecham. 'Think about all the wonderful things about performing. Think about having fun with your friends and making the concert enjoyable for all the children at school.'

'Maybe,' I said hesitantly. 'But I don't want to make an idiot of myself again. I don't want the other kids to laugh at us.'

Mrs Beecham dismissed my concern with a little huff and a wave of her hand.

'Better people think that you tried hard than that you couldn't be bothered to try at all,' she said. 'The difference between doing something badly and doing something well is just practice.'

Mrs Beecham had told me something like this before when I had been struggling to learn the steps in Miss Demi's dance class. I had taken some of her advice then and it had definitely helped me. Maybe she was right again? The judges were giving us a second chance. I imagined how excited Cici and Charlie would be. I felt I owed it to my friends to try.

'Okay,' I agreed. 'I'll talk to the girls and let you know.'

Mrs Beecham took my hand and squeezed it. 'Remember, just think positive thoughts,' she said. 'Our artistic director always said "*act* as though you're confident and you'll look as though you *are* confident". Otherwise known as fake it 'til you make it!'

That made me laugh. 'Thanks, Mrs Beecham,' I said. 'I'll ask the girls now.'

As I expected, the girls were super-excited that we had a second chance to perform. I told them everything that Mrs Beecham had said. We needed concert costumes and we needed them fast. We spent the rest of recess huddled in a corner talking about what we had to do. Lunchtime was spent in the library researching costume ideas.

There was nothing for it but to call an emergency Sassy Sisters meeting. This time we chose

Cici's house so we could take advantage of her mum's storeroom full of fabrics. The four of us raced there straight after school, stopping in at the cafe and Meg's yacht so we could let our parents know what we were planning. Charlie phoned her mum from Cici's place.

Cici's mum was out at a client fitting, so Cici phoned her to get permission to raid her material store. Luckily, Nathalie said we could help ourselves to anything we needed. Cici's dad was home, cooking in the kitchen with Cici's brother, Will. Eric was teaching Will how to make prawn dumplings with dipping sauce. The kitchen was filled with the sweet and spicy smells of brown sugar, sesame, soy sauce and chilli. Will was frowning with concentration as he wrapped the delicate dumplings.

The four of us gathered in the sunny studio, standing around the big antique table that Nathalie used as a desk. The room had French doors that opened onto a paved terrace with star jasmine growing over the trellis and terracotta pots overflowing with pink geraniums.

One wall was covered with a giant black fabric mood board, with fashion photographs, swatches of material and pencil sketches pinned up. Two headless mannequins stood in one corner, wearing dresses in bold floral prints.

We had printed a collection of photos of costumes that we'd found on the internet at lunchtime. Meg spread the prints out on the table.

'Which one do you like best?' asked Meg.

'I think this one's my favourite,' said Cici, tapping one of the pictures. 'It's fun and colourful and looks simple to make.'

The photo showed four girls posing closely together, wearing black T-shirts with black leggings and sneakers. Over the top of their leggings, each girl wore a fluffy tutu in different rainbow colours. On their heads they wore tiaras covered in sparkly diamantes.

'Black leggings and tops will be super-easy,' I said. 'We all have those.'

'The tutus are adorable,' said Charlie. 'But can we really make them ourselves?'

'Absolutely,' said Cici, pulling out a set of instructions she had copied from the website. 'We don't even need to sew them. All we need is a wide ribbon to go around our waists, and then strips of tulle to knot onto the ribbon in whatever colour we fancy.'

We all read Cici's instructions.

CICI'S GUIDE TO MAKING YOUR OWN TUTU

1. Using a soft measuring tape, measure around your waist. Then measure the length you would like the tutu to be.

2. Choose your colours and materials. You will need tulle for the skirt and wide ribbon for the waistband.

3. Cut a length of ribbon for the waistband. This should be 40 centimetres longer than the measurement around your waist. Tie a knot 20 centimetres from each end of the ribbon so you know where your waistband finishes. The extra length is to tie a bow.

4. Cut your tulle into strips. Each strip should be twice the length that you want your skirt to be (e.g. if you want your tutu to be 30 centimetres long, make sure the strips are 60 centimetres

long). For an extra fluffy tutu cut lots of narrow strips.

5. Fold your tulle strips in half. Attach each strip onto the ribbon waistband by pulling the long tails around the ribbon and through the loop created by the folded tulle. Pull the tails all the way through to tighten the loop into a knot that sits flat against the waistband ribbon.

6. Continue adding strips until you have filled the whole length of the waistband in between the marker knots.

7. Tie the tutu around your waist with a bow at the back. Or to be super-stylish, have the bow at the front and just to one side. Easy-peasy!

Cici found a measuring tape and some pairs of fabric scissors in the top drawer of the desk. 'Come with me, girls,' she said.

The room next to Nathalie's studio was a large storage room with floor-to-ceiling shelves stacked with plastic tubs, cardboard boxes and roll upon roll of fabrics in every colour you could imagine. There were also rollaway racks laden with clothes on hangers. It was a fashion-ista's treasure trove.

Cici filled our arms with rolls of tulle, spools of satin ribbon, a box of silk flowers and remnants of iridescent silky fabrics in shim-mering silver, icy-blue and opal-white.

'I love this peacock-blue,' said Meg, stroking the stiff tulle with her fingers.

'I can't decide between this mossy-green and the hot-pink,' said Charlie, as we walked back into the studio.

'You could mix two or three colours together if you want,' said Cici with a grin. 'Let's experiment.'

We laid the different tulle colours out on the table and mixed and matched them with various ribbons, colours and decorations until we had each decided what we wanted. Cici was our fashion advisor.

In the end Meg chose summery colours of opal-white and yellow, with a cluster of yellow and pink frangipanis at the waist. Charlie went with green to match the colour of her eyes, with three blue cornflowers pinned on the waistband. Cici chose bold, flame colours of red, orange and yellow, which looked dramatic with her black hair. I couldn't decide. In the end I chose sea colours of turquoise and peacock-blue with glints of shimmering silver.

Now it was time to make our skirts. Firstly, we each had to cut a long strip of satin ribbon. Mine was cream. The ribbon had to be long enough to go around our waist and then tie in a pretty bow at the back. We measured the ribbon and tied a tiny knot on each side to show our waist measurements.

Then we had to cut our tulle. We used the measuring tape to see how long we wanted our skirts to be. Cici wanted hers quite short and frothy, whereas Meg wanted hers to be longer and feathery.

We cut the tulle into lots of narrow strips. It took ages!

'Remember to measure twice and cut once,' Cici warned us. 'We don't want to make mistakes and waste the material.'

Then Cici showed us how to attach the tulle strips onto the waistband. Each strip was folded in half to create a loop. We neatly threaded the ends of the tulle around the ribbon and through the loop, securing them to the waistband. This was the really fun part as the tutu took shape quickly. When the ribbon was completely full of tulle strips between the two marker knots, we tried them on.

The skirts were stiff and springy, floating about as we twirled and pranced.

'They look brilliant,' I said, spinning in a pirouette, just to see my tutu swirl out.

Charlie jumped up and down, playing air guitar.

'I can't believe we made them ourselves,' said Meg, capering around the room. 'They look so professional.'

'Not quite,' said Cici, examining each tutu. 'Just a couple of finishing touches to go.'

Cici used safety pins to attach the artificial frangipanis to the front of Meg's tutu, then the three blue cornflowers to Charlie's waistband. With mine, she knotted on some floaty pieces of silver material, which glimmered in the light as I moved.

'Perfect,' said Cici. 'Now we just have to decide on our headwear.'

We packed up all the materials and put them away in the storeroom. All the snips and scraps went in the bin and the scissors away in the top drawer. Then, when everything was back to normal, we went to Cici's room with its filmy white curtains, polka-dot quilt cover and the quirky white reindeer head on the wall. A long bank of built-in wardrobes took up the far wall. This is where Cici kept all her fabulous fashion. She opened a drawer that was neatly stacked with hair accessories – ribbons, clips, head-bands, tiaras, scrunchies and flower crowns. Her fingers flew over the treasure trove, picking out several items that she thought would work.

'Help yourself, girls,' said Cici, placing them on the dressing table. We tried on different headbands with our hair all flowing and loose. It was hard to choose.

At last we decided on a garland of blue cornflowers for Charlie, frangipanis for Meg, a circlet of tiny pearls for me and a diamante tiara for Cici the Flame Queen. We looked at ourselves in Cici's full-length mirror.

'You all look gorgeous,' said Charlie.

'So do you,' I said.

Cici put on her most theatrical voice. 'Ladies and gentlemen – I give you the Sassy Sisters!'

I felt a thrill of excitement.

Cici picked up her guitar. 'Let's do it.'

My costume made me feel completely different. When Cici started to play the opening chords, I grabbed her hairbrush off the dressing table, opened my mouth and sang with gusto.

It was just like all the times when we mucked around together, singing our favourite songs for fun. If only I could capture this feeling when we sang in the concert tomorrow.

We could be brilliant. Now we just needed to come up with an idea to make our stage presence sparkle.

CHAPTER 11

HARRY'S MAGIC BOX

The solution came to me in a flash of inspiration in the middle of the night. I sat up suddenly and bumped my head on the caravan roof. Oh, I couldn't wait to sleep in a proper bedroom!

My idea came from Harry asking Bella to be in his magic act. The solution was simple. What if we combined our 'Kira Dreaming' singing act with the Fabulous Five's 'Kira Dreaming' dancing and gymnastics routine? Tash, of course, couldn't dance but perhaps she could sit on a stool and sing with us.

Surely the other girls could adapt their performance to fill in the section in the middle which had been for Tash's dramatic solo. The gym girls were all beautiful dancers and skilled at memorising choreography. I was certain they could improvise.

I couldn't wait to get to school to ask the other girls what they thought.

When I woke up again in the morning, the caravan was strangely quiet. Mum, Bella, Harry and Summer were all gone. Mum had probably gone to the cafe as usual. She must have taken Smudge with her in her crate. But where were the others?

I padded out to the garden in my pyjamas and bare feet. Sounds of muffled laughter came from the garage. I recognised Bella's giggle. But what were they doing in the garage so early in the morning?

I opened the garage door and went inside. Papa, Harry and Summer were standing beside a fabulous contraption. Summer rushed to greet me, licking my bare toes and ankles with puppy kisses.

In the middle of the garage was a rectangular box, taller than me. It was painted in a deep midnight-blue with mystical silver stars and moons scattered over it. Harry was standing in front of the box, wearing his top hat and magician's cape over his blue pyjamas. Bella was nowhere to be seen. This must be the magic disappearing box that Papa and Harry had built together.

'Good morning, Pippa,' said Papa with a warm smile. 'Have you come to see Harry's latest creation?'

'It looks professional,' I replied. 'Is Bella inside it?'

'Yep,' said Harry. 'Bella, I'm opening the door to show Pippa.'

He took hold of a silver handle on the front of the box and pulled. The side of the box opened on hinges like a door. Bella was standing inside the box dressed in her orange-and-black tiger onesie.

She jiggled up and down with excitement. 'It works, Pippa. It really works.'

'Come out, Bella, so we can show Pippa the act,' said Harry.

Bella skipped out of the box and stood beside me. The inside of the box was painted black, making it look shadowy and mysterious.

'Ladies and gentlemen,' said Harry, in his magician stage voice. 'As you can see, the box is completely empty.'

'There's no gentle-*men*, only gentle-*man*,' interrupted Bella, pointing at Papa.

Harry ignored her.

'Now, I need a volunteer from the audience,'

said Harry, standing in front of the box and waving his wand about. 'I will make that person magically disappear.'

Bella stuck her hand in the air and jumped up and down. 'Me. Me. Choose me.'

'Could you please come to the stage, young lady,' said Harry, beckoning with his hand.

Bella bounded up to stand beside him.

'And what's your name?' asked Harry, taking her hand and shaking it.

'You already know my name,' said Bella, pouting. 'I'm your sister.'

Harry glared at Bella.

'My name's Isabella Hamilton,' said Bella, meekly.

'Now, don't be frightened, Isabella,' said Harry. 'I am Harry the Marvellous Magician and I am going to make you disappear, but I almost always manage to bring people back.'

'Okay,' said Bella. 'I'm not scared.'

'Step into the box,' ordered Harry.

Bella skipped inside the box and turned around so she was facing us. She waved and jiggled. Harry closed the door with a great flourish, shutting Bella inside. He took his wand and gestured in the air.

'Abracadabra. Alakazam!' cried Harry. 'Make this marvellous maiden magically melt away.'

He tapped the door with his wand three times. Then he flung the door open. *'Tada.'*

The box inside was completely empty. Bella had disappeared.

'Bravo,' said Papa, clapping his hands. 'Perfectly done.'

'Where is she?' I asked, thinking fast. 'I know. There's another door at the back of the box and she's escaped. I bet she's hiding there.'

I ran around the back of the box but Bella wasn't crouched there. Summer sniffed around the base of the box and barked. She was as confused as I was.

I came back to the front of the box. Harry preened, looking very pleased with himself.

'If you're quite ready?' he asked.

I nodded.

He tapped the box once and opened the door. There was no one there. Harry smacked his forehead in fake frustration.

'Of course. I forgot the magic spell.'

He closed the door, waved his wand and cried, 'Abracadabra. Alakazam! Make this magical maiden return again.'

Harry opened the door. There was Bella, grinning from ear to ear. She pounced out of the box with a roar.

Harry and Bella took a bow. Papa and I both clapped our hardest.

'What a fabulous act,' I said. 'That's even better than what you did at the audition.'

'I know,' said Harry. 'Bella's done a great job of mastering the illusion.'

Bella beamed with happiness.

'Well, that's enough rehearsal for now,' said Papa. 'It's time you three got dressed for school.

I'm going to make you my famous poached eggs and avocado on toast, so don't be too long.'

The three of us scrambled back to the caravan to get ready.

Bella and Harry were ready first and they ran off to eat breakfast in the cottage. I was just leaving the caravan myself when I heard a funny vibrating noise coming from the shelf near Mum and Bella's double bed.

Mum had left her phone behind.

I looked at the display. It read Andrew Hamilton. My heart sank. It was Dad again.

Should I answer it? I still felt angry with him.

It seemed as though the phone vibrated more urgently. I picked it up.

'Hello? Dad?' I said.

'Pippa, sweetheart. Is that you?' came my dad's familiar voice.

'Yes,' I said.

There was an awkward pause.

'What are you doing?' asked Dad, trying to be cheery.

'Getting ready for school,' I said. 'Papa's just made breakfast.'

'Oh,' said Dad. 'And what about Bella and Harry?'

'They're getting ready for school too,' I said.

'I see. I was hoping to speak to them.' Dad was sounding desperate again.

'They're in the cottage,' I said. 'Eating poached eggs on toast.' Then I felt sorry for Dad. He was trying. He missed us too.

So I decided to tell Dad about Harry's magic box that he'd made with Papa and the disappearing act he'd practised with Bella.

'That sounds marvellous,' said Dad, wistfully. 'I wish I could see that.'

'It's for the VIP concert on Friday,' I said. 'And I'm performing a song with my friends.'

'I'm sure you'll be fantastic,' said Dad.

'Well, the audition didn't go very well,' I admitted. I told Dad all about my stage fright.

'Poor Pippa,' he said. 'That sounds like a total disaster.'

'It was,' I said. 'And I'm scared I'll freeze all over again on Friday.'

'I used to get terribly nervous before all my presentations,' confessed Dad. That surprised me! When he had his own business, Dad had to present important information to clients all the time. I'd often seen him practising in front of the mirror at home. He'd always seemed calm and confident.

'Did you?' I asked. 'Harry said you told him to imagine everyone in the audience was sitting in their underwear.'

Dad laughed. 'Harry told you that, did he? Well, I have a couple of other tricks that might help you.'

'Like what?' I asked.

'I find it helps to do some exercise before the performance, like stretching or going for a quick walk to burn up all that nervous energy,' suggested Dad. 'Take lots of deep breaths to help calm yourself down just before you start.'

'That makes sense,' I said.

Dad paused on the other end of the line. 'I know this sounds funny, but the thing that helps me the most is to stand really tall with my arms and legs stretched out like a starfish. Can you do that?'

I wrinkled my nose in total disbelief. Then I held the phone to one ear while I planted my feet wide apart and stretched the other arm up in the air. I stretched myself taller.

'Yes, I'm doing it,' I said.

'Make yourself as tall as you possibly can and say to yourself, "I am ten feet tall and bolder than I've ever been. I'm going to smash this performance!"'

I stretched even taller. 'I am ten feet tall and bolder than I have ever been. I'm going to *smash* this performance!'

I laughed out loud to imagine how ridiculous I must look and sound.

'And that's the secret of how to turn yourself from a timid mouse with stage fright into a superhero performer,' said Dad.

Dad was right. I did feel stronger and more confident.

'Thanks, Dad,' I said, and I really meant it. 'I'd better go. Papa's eggs will be getting cold.'

'Bye, Pippa,' said Dad. 'I love you.'

'Love you, too, Dad,' I said. I hung up, but before I went to the cottage for breakfast I decided there was one thing I needed to do.

I grabbed my notebook and wrote myself a list.

TOP TIPS TO SMASH STAGE FRIGHT

1. Mrs Beecham says: 'Fake it 'til you make it.' Act confident and you'll be confident.
2. Harry says: 'Imagine everyone is in their underwear.'
3. Dad says: 'Go for a walk. Take deep breaths. Then make yourself into a starfish and say, "I am ten feet tall and bolder than I have ever been. I'm going to smash this performance!"'
4. I say: 'Laugh!' It does make you feel better.

As soon as I saw Charlie, Cici and Meg in the playground at school, I told them my idea of inviting the Fabulous Five to join our act. Luckily they all agreed it was the perfect solution.

I saw Olivia and Willow across the playground arm in arm. I jogged towards them.

'Olivia,' I called. 'Willow. Can you wait a moment?'

The girls stopped.

'I hear that you and the others are taking our place in the concert,' said Olivia with a sniff. She didn't look very happy about the idea.

'Yes, we are,' I said. I thought for a moment, wondering what to say next. 'But the judges are worried that our act isn't quite good enough.'

Olivia looked chirpier at this news. 'I'm surprised they asked you, to be honest. I suppose they didn't want to choose your little sister. That was definitely one of the worst songs I've ever heard.'

Olivia was right. Bella's performance had been excruciating but I bristled in defence of my sister all the same. While we seemed to get on better most of the time now, Olivia still had an amazing talent for saying things that upset me. I wondered if I really wanted to go ahead with my plan.

'I'm sure you guys will be great,' said Willow hurriedly.

I decided to ignore Oliva's gibe.

'I have an idea for the concert tomorrow,' I said. 'An idea to make our act really outstanding. But we need your help.'

Olivia and Willow listened as I outlined my plan. Willow nodded her head. Olivia looked unimpressed to begin with, but then I could see that even she was excited.

'All right,' said Olivia. 'We'll do it.'

CHAPTER 12

THE CONCERT

Friday morning dawned hot and bright. All of us were awake super-early. I jumped out of my bunk, jangling with nerves. This time I forced myself to eat my poached egg on toast. In the bathroom, I took a few deep breaths and stretched myself into a starfish to practise.

Papa and Mimi drove us to school. We had a full carload with Harry's magical disappearing box, plus all the costumes and props. Bella had her tiger onesie costume. Harry had his magician outfit and magic bag. I was wearing my black singlet, leggings and sneakers with the rest of my costume packed in a tote bag. The concert was planned to start first thing after the morning bell.

Papa and Harry carried his box inside and stored it behind the stage. A number of students were on hand, dressed all in black, to help set up props for the different acts.

Parents, grandparents and friends of the school were all invited to come along for the special performance. Mimi and Papa were the first ones to take their seats.

Then Mum and Zoe arrived together. Mum gave me an extra-big hug. 'I'm so proud of you, Pipkin. I know you'll be fantastic.'

I hugged her back. 'Thanks, Mum.' Then I turned to Zoe.

'I didn't know you were coming, Zoe,' I said.

'There's no way I'd miss it,' she replied. 'We arranged for my friend Lisa to mind the cafe for an hour or so. But it looks like all our customers are here anyway!'

We looked around as the hall filled with people. All my friends' parents were there, including Nathalie and Eric, Charlie's mum, Jodie, and her stepfather, Dave, Mariana and Phillip, and Willow's mum, Caitlin. I felt sad when I thought that my dad couldn't be here to see us all perform.

The parents all took their seats on chairs up the back of the hall. The front row was reserved for our VIP visitors. The students all sat cross-legged on the floor at the front. Mum went over to chat to Nathalie and Eric.

Zoe took out her phone. 'I'm going to stand at the side, in that little alcove near the front, so I can take lots of photos of you all.'

This suddenly gave me an idea. 'Zoe, do you think you could do me a really big favour, please?' I asked. I glanced over to make sure Mum was still busy chatting.

'Sure, Pippa,' said Zoe. 'What do you need?'

'Do you think you could video our song and Harry and Bella's magic show? I didn't want to ask Mum to do it.'

Zoe nodded. 'Of course I can. Any particular reason?'

'I want to send the video to my dad in Switzerland so he can see us,' I said. 'Harry's worked really hard and Bella's so excited, and I know they secretly wish he could be here to see it.'

Zoe winked at me, her silver earrings swinging. 'Consider it done.'

Charlie stuck her head around the door and beckoned to me. 'Hurry up, Pippa,' she called. 'We need to get ready.'

At once I felt the nerves slam me in the stomach. I felt sick with anxiety. *Not again*, I thought, as Charlie disappeared towards the changing rooms. I followed her slowly, dragging my feet. Then I remembered what Dad had said, so I ran instead, taking big

187

deep breaths, hoping to burn up some excess energy.

Two classrooms near the hall had been turned into changing rooms for the concert. One for the girls and one for the boys. Charlie went inside first. I stopped outside the door and I glanced behind me. No one was around.

I stretched myself up as high as I could in a wide-armed, wide-legged starfish position. Inside my head I roared, 'I am ten feet tall and bolder than I have ever been. I'm going to *smash* this performance!' I closed my eyes and took some deep breaths.

Charlie's voice broke into my reverie. 'Pippa, are you all right?'

I blushed fiery-pink and opened my eyes. 'Dad says it's a good technique for smashing stage fright.'

'Excellent,' said Charlie. She sprung into a starfish. 'Let's do it together!'

We stood outside the door in our identical

starfish positions. I giggled at the absurdity of what we were doing. Charlie giggled back.

'Feeling better?' she asked.

'Lots,' I said. 'We're going to be brilliant!'

'Let's get dressed then,' suggested Charlie.

Olivia, Jemila, Willow and Sienna were just inside the door doing gymnastics warm-ups in their leotards and leggings. Tash sat on a chair, supervising. I gave them a thumbs-up sign. Cici and Meg were at the back of the classroom, looking gorgeous in their colourful tutus.

'There you are,' said Cici. 'We were starting to get worried you might have run away!'

'No, I was just preparing,' I said with a reassuring smile.

Cici handed me my fluffy sea-blue tutu. I wrapped it around my waist and tied the ribbon at the back, over my leggings.

Charlie helped me pin my pearl circlet in place. Then I helped her with her garland of cornflowers, pinning it firmly over her hair.

Cici pulled out a pale-pink lip gloss from her bag with a flourish. 'To help with nervous dry lips and make you super-confident.'

I took the lid off the lip gloss and ran a slick over my lips. 'Just the trick,' I said. 'Now I'm invincible.'

Mrs Marshall appeared at the door. 'All right, girls. Are you ready? It's time to take your seats.'

We bustled through the side door and into the hall. The other performers were already seated at the front, dressed in their costumes.

We wriggled and fidgeted with excitement as we sat cross-legged on the floor. The boys were sitting behind us.

Alex leaned forward.

'Good luck up there, Pippa,' he whispered. 'Sing hard. You'll be awesome.'

I smiled back at him. 'Thanks, Alex.'

Our principal, Mrs Black, took the microphone. 'Ladies and gentlemen, boys and girls, can you please stand while our very special guests from the mainland join us.'

Everyone stood up. We all craned our heads around to stare at the VIP guests. Two men and three women entered the hall. They were all wearing suits and were accompanied by two police officers, who stood at the back door. The five VIPs walked to the front row where Mrs Marshall showed them to their reserved seats next to Mrs Beecham.

Our curiosity was satisfied in just a moment when Mrs Black introduced them. 'Kira Cove Primary School would like to give a very warm welcome to the Honourable Kate Macnamara, State Minister for Education. We are so honoured to have you here on Kira Island to visit our school.'

Everyone clapped enthusiastically. The education minister was in the centre, dressed in a scarlet suit. She waved and smiled at the students. 'Thank you, Mrs Black. I am delighted to be here.'

Mrs Black continued. 'We also welcome our local member of parliament, Ms Li Ying, together with representatives from the Department of Education, Mr King, Ms Muller and Mr Kumar. Can you please give them a big round of applause?'

We all clapped again.

'Now let the performances begin,' said Mrs Black. She handed the microphone to Mrs Marshall, who was the MC, and took her place beside the ministerial party.

Cici passed down a stack of printed programs. I glanced at one.

KIRA COVE PRIMARY SCHOOL TALENT SHOWCASE

1. The Kindy Kitty-cats
2. Kira Cove Senior Band
3. The Hip-Hop Boyz
4. Harry the Marvellous Magician
5. 'Kira Dreaming' – The Sassy Sisters

The first act was the Kindy Kitty-cats, jigging to the kitty-cat song. The kids made heaps of mistakes but they were so cute that it didn't really matter.

The little girl with no front teeth managed to get halfway through the dance before she realised that there was a huge audience watching her. Then she stood staring at the minister, sucking her thumb.

When the music finished, the dance teacher, Miss Demi, had to take her by the hand and lead her off stage.

The kitty-cats were followed by the senior band, in their crisp white uniforms, who played a swinging dance tune. Many of the parents were tapping their feet to the music. Then Alex and the boys danced their hearts out to their hip-hop routine. Their floor spins were spectacular. I clapped as hard as I could when they finished. So far the concert had been a resounding success.

The fourth act was Harry the Marvellous Magician. Harry swept onto the stage in his cloak and top hat, looking every bit the professional performer. Four stagehands carried the midnight-blue magic box painted with silver stars and moons and placed it in the centre of the stage.

Harry gave his opening spiel, then called for volunteers from the audience. Lots of students raised their hand, calling out 'Pick me! Pick me!'.

'Harry didn't have an assistant on Tuesday,' whispered Cici.

'No, but he's doing a new act,' I replied. 'Wait till you see it. It's fantastic.'

Of course, I wasn't at all surprised when he selected Bella, dressed in her tiger onesie, to come up on the stage to be his assistant.

For the first act, he strode up the central aisle and made the minister's mobile phone disappear, much to the consternation of the two police officers, but he returned it a few minutes later with a flourishing bow.

Harry 'lost' the blue chiffon scarf in his magic fist and Bella managed to 'find' it in the collar of our local member, Ms Ying. We all craned our heads to watch. I was thrilled to see the State Minister for Education applauding and chuckling with delight. The audience oohed and aahed over his disappearing silver ball trick and laughed when Bella pulled the toy rabbit out of his top hat.

'For our final act,' said Harry, 'I'm going to make this terrible tiger disappear. Young lady, would you mind stepping inside my magic box?'

He opened the midnight-blue door to reveal the black-painted interior. Bella made a great show of swaggering into the shadowy box. She turned around to face the audience and gave a cheeky grin. Harry closed the door, took his wand and waved it in the air.

'Abracadabra. Alakazam!' cried Harry. 'Make this maiden magically melt away.'

He tapped the box three times with his wand. Then he flung the door open. '*Tada!*'

Inside the box was completely empty. Bella had disappeared.

'*Ooh*,' cooed the audience.

'How did he do that?' whispered Meg.

'*Magic*,' I replied, waggling my eyebrows.

Once again, Harry 'forgot' to say the magic words so the box was still empty. But on the third attempt, when Harry opened the door, Bella bounced out of the box, beaming from ear to ear.

The crowd went crazy, hooting and clapping.

Harry and Bella bowed, then bowed again as the applause continued. My siblings had done a brilliant routine. I felt my heart bursting with pride.

'It's our turn,' whispered Meg, as Harry and Bella left the stage. I'd been so busy enjoying the other performances that I hadn't had time to get nervous yet. At once the familiar butterflies started doing cartwheels in my tummy.

The helpers cleared away the magic box and set up a stool in the centre of the stage as well as our microphones. I took a few deep breaths. *Have courage*, I told myself. *Act confident and you'll be confident.*

Charlie and Cici grabbed their guitars, wearing them across their chests on long shoulder straps. I followed the girls up the stairs and behind the curtains. I stretched myself out into my starfish position and whispered my mantra to myself. *I'm ten feet tall and bolder than I've ever been . . .*

'And our final act is . . . the Sassy Sisters,' called Mrs Marshall.

Charlie took my hand. 'You'll be great,' she assured me.

'It'll be fun!' I replied.

The four of us ran onstage in our frothy tutus. The audience cheered. This time, we stood in the centre of the stage in front of the lone stool. Charlie counted us in. 'One, two, three . . .'

In the audience I could see Mrs Beecham waving at me. Mum was in the front row of seats and she blew me a kiss. Zoe stood to the right against the wall and pointed to her phone to show me she was videoing. She gave me a thumbs-up sign. I felt a big bubble of happiness well up as we started to sing, jigging and swaying to the music.

Halfway through the first verse, the door at the back of the hall burst open. Four girls in black leotards and hot-pink tutus pranced through the door, waving their arms in the air in time to our music. It was Olivia, Willow, Sienna and Jemila with broad grins on their faces. We had made extra tutus for them yesterday afternoon. Olivia led them in single file, tumbling and cartwheeling down the central aisle through the middle of the audience.

When they reached the front, the group split, skipping up the stairs on either side of the stage, two by two. The girls began to dance behind us. Olivia disappeared for a moment behind the side curtains, then she helped Tash hobble out to sit on the stool in between us. Tash's left leg was still swollen, wrapped with bandages under her leggings and tutu.

Tash beamed as she began to sing the words with us. We sang the last verse to the song, 'As the summer sun goes down, happy Kira Dreaming . . .'

Olivia, Willow, Sienna and Jemila flung themselves into a series of cartwheels in a giant circle around us. Tash twitched as though she was itching to join them.

The crowd roared and clapped as we finished our song. Charlie had been right. It was fun!

Charlie, Cici, Meg and I crowded together in a big bear hug, our arms wrapped tight around each other, smiling with relief. Then

Tash, Willow, Sienna, Jemila and finally Olivia swarmed around us, joining the embrace.

And with that our concert was over. We'd done it.

Afterwards was a confusion of congratulations and chatting. All the performers were invited to have a special morning tea to meet the minister and the other VIPs.

The State Minister for Education shook hands with us all, one by one, murmuring compliments about our performances. Then she gave a short speech, explaining that she was here as part of a study tour visiting several remote schools.

'I've spent time in many schools around the state but that was the best talent quest I've ever seen,' Ms Macnamara said, beaming around at all of us. 'You should all be very proud of yourselves.'

Then she looked straight over at Meg, Charlie, Cici and me.

'But I must say, I particularly enjoyed the singing and dancing performance of my new favourite song, "Kira Dreaming",' she said. 'I am so impressed that a small school like this, on a tiny tropical island, could produce such a professional performance. It is a huge credit to the students and teachers of Kira Cove School. Well done all of you.'

CHAPTER 13

TOWER-WARMING PARTY

Before we knew it, it was Friday afternoon and the start of the weekend. Today we planned an extra special Sassy Sisters club meeting at the Beach Shack. Bella, Harry and I went straight from school to the cafe, all still wearing our costumes.

Zoe was out the front of the cafe, writing up the specials on the chalkboard. I asked her if she could send Dad the videos that she had taken on her phone. She winked and said it was next on her list.

Inside, we checked on tiny Smudge. She was in her crate, up on a sideboard out of the way, where she could see everyone coming and going. Our kitten already looked so much better. Her coat was now black and glossy, and she had put on weight. Smudge no longer cowered in her crate, but scampered over to the door to rub her cheek against my finger.

I carefully lifted her out and snuggled her. Last night had been the first time we'd been allowed to cuddle Smudge, but only for a few minutes. Her fur felt soft and velvety under my chin. A purr rumbled deep in her chest.

'Hello, Smudge,' I whispered to her. 'I'm so glad you came to live with us.'

Mum noticed me cuddling the kitten. 'Pipkin, why don't you take her to your room and let her have a good run around up there with the door closed? Caitlin said that today we could start to let her out as long as it's in a contained space.'

Harry and Bella followed as I carried the crate upstairs and put it inside my empty bedroom. I closed the door and let Smudge out of her crate. Harry and Bella took turns cuddling her on the floor while I went upstairs to the tower room to make some special preparations for today's meeting. When I was done, I went back downstairs to wait for the girls.

As I clattered down the stairs, I heard the phone ringing, then Mum's voice as she answered it.

Mum paused for a moment, then called me over and handed me the phone. She had a funny look on her face and her voice sounded a little wobbly. 'It's for you, Pipkin. It's your dad.'

'Oh,' I said. 'Hello, Dad?'

This time Dad's voice sounded a long way away and rather crackly. 'Good morning, sweetheart – I mean, I suppose it's nearly good evening there now . . .'

'We just finished school,' I said. 'It's Friday afternoon.'

'Thanks for sending me those videos,' said Dad. 'Harry and Bella's magic performance was fabulous. And I was so proud of you. I loved watching you sing with your friends.'

My heart blossomed with pride. 'Thanks, Dad. Your suggestions really helped. Charlie and I made ourselves laugh being giant starfish just before we went on stage.'

I saw Mum watching me. Suddenly I didn't feel so chatty. I talked to Dad for a minute more and then we said goodbye.

'I didn't know you sent your dad a video of the concert today,' said Mum.

I felt awkward and somehow guilty. 'I asked Zoe to video us,' I admitted. 'I didn't want to bother you about it.'

Mum gave me a hug. 'That was a really special thing to do, Pipkin,' she said. 'I should have thought of it myself.'

Mum's reaction surprised me. I thought she might have been upset or hurt or even angry.

'You're not upset with me?' I asked.

Mum shook her head. 'Of course not. I must admit, I've been avoiding calls from your father and that was wrong of me. I shouldn't have, but I was feeling tired and busy with everything going on. And Bella was so upset last time I couldn't really face it. But it's important you kids talk to your dad and let him know what's going on in your lives.'

That was a relief. I hated the feeling that somehow we had to choose sides between Mum and Dad. I gave Mum a hug. I snuggled in tight, breathing in her familiar warm scent.

Just then Charlie, Cici and Meg arrived, calling hellos and carrying presents. Cici was carrying an enormous box which was nearly as big as she was. I wondered what it could possibly hold.

'What's that?' I asked, burning up with curiosity.

'A surprise,' said Cici, with a huge grin as she put the box down on the floor.

'Lots of surprises,' added Meg.

Charlie and Meg placed their presents on top of the box.

'Presents?' I asked. 'Why have you brought presents?'

'For the tower-warming party,' said Charlie. 'We wanted to celebrate our new super-*quiet*, super-special meeting place!'

I did a little jig of excitement. 'Let's go up!'

'I've packed a basket of goodies so you can have a picnic upstairs,' said Mum, handing me a wicker basket covered with a cloth. 'I thought you needed some extra special treats to celebrate your amazing success today.'

'Thanks so much, Mum,' I said.

The four of us went upstairs to my room. Smudge was sitting on the window seat with Harry and Bella, but when she saw the three strangers she ran and hid in her open crate.

'She's still a little shy,' I explained to the girls. 'But she'll get used to you.'

The girls oohed and aahed over Smudge as she skulked in her crate, then we climbed the ladder up to the tower, leaving the cupboard door open down below. We had to help Cici haul up the big box, but it was surprisingly light. I carried up the basket that Mum had filled with special treats for our tower-warming party.

'Pippa,' said Meg, gazing around the tower room. 'It looks incredible.'

'Doesn't it?' I replied with immense satisfaction. I was surprised all over again by how good it looked painted fresh and white. My seafoam-green fruit-crate shelves were installed around one half of the wall, tied together with brown string. I'd stacked a pile of my favourite books on the shelves and popped some pens and pencils in a jam jar. Another jam jar held purple agapanthus, white orchids and feathery green ferns. I'd thrown a white cloth over my fruit-crate table and spread a faded, round rug in the centre of the room that I'd borrowed from Mimi.

The girls crowded around me.

'And now for the tower-warming presents,' said Cici. 'We each made you something, plus my mum sent a present as well.'

The first present I opened was from Nathalie. She had made us a set of four puffy, square floor cushions in different fabrics. They were my favourite ocean colours: turquoise, aqua, sea-foam-green and ocean-blue. Now we had something to sit on for our meetings. We each jumped on a cushion and sat cross-legged.

'These are gorgeous, Cici,' I said, bouncing up and down. 'Your mum is *soooo* clever to make these.'

Cici handed me a tiny parcel. 'And this is from me. I hope you like it.'

Inside was a length of beautiful bunting in

similar sea shades that Cici had sewed onto white ribbon. The triangles of fabric were in solid colours and a variety of patterns – stripes, polka dots and stars. Cici had also brought some brass hooks.

'We can screw the hooks into the wall up high and drape the bunting above the windows,' she suggested. She held the bunting up wide so I could see how it would look.

'I love it,' I said.

'I made you something too,' said Meg. I tore the wrapping off. Meg's present was a photo board covered in pale-green fabric, pinned with a collection of square photographs that Meg had taken of us having fabulous fun together. There were photos of us kayaking, playing with Summer, riding skateboards, pulling silly faces with Ruby Starr and even one of us dressed in our tutus from the concert this morning. Meg had glued on shells and starfish to give it a beachy feel.

We all gushed over the photos. 'This is so special,' I said. 'And you've even included my favourite photo of us at the opening of the cafe.'

I propped the photo board up on the top shelf of my bookcase. The last present was from Charlie.

'Careful. It's a bit delicate,' she said.

Charlie had made me a mobile from drift-wood, string and a variety of seashells including pipis, cockles, clams and scallops.

'It's exquisite,' I said, holding it up to see how the shells spun in the breeze.

'And Mum helped me make this,' said Charlie. It was a rustic sign made from fence palings with our Sassy Sisters' motto painted in large letters:

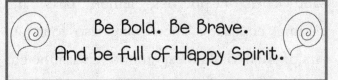

Be Bold. Be Brave.
And be full of Happy Spirit.

Charlie propped the sign against the wall and hung her mobile from an old hook on the ceiling. Cici draped the bunting across the window. We stood in the middle of the tower room and spun around. Our tower room was truly beautiful.

Charlie sat down on her cushion.

'As President of the Sassy Sisters, I vote that we tackle some very important business,' she said.

'What's that?' I asked, taking my own cushion and gazing around once more at the transformation we'd wrought.

'Afternoon tea,' said Charlie. 'I'm starving.'

Meg took the cloth off the top of the basket. Nestled inside was a two-tiered plate stand laden with chicken-and-lettuce finger sandwiches, raspberries, lemon tarts and caramel cupcakes. There were also four jam jars of Mango Madness smoothie with the lids screwed on to stop them spilling.

I lifted the cake stand out of the basket and onto my fruit-crate table. Meg handed everyone a jam jar.

'*Tada*,' I said. 'Afternoon tea is served.'

Just then a little black-and-white head popped up through the hole in the floor.

'Look, it's Smudge,' I cried. 'She climbed up the ladder all by herself. Clever kitty-kins.'

Smudge looked at us with her big green eyes and mewed.

'Aaww,' said Charlie. 'She's adorable.'

Smudge mustered up the courage to come the rest of the way up the ladder. She scampered over to my lap and snuggled into my arms, purring loudly.

'Time to celebrate,' announced Cici. She screwed the lid off her jar of Mango Madness and raised it in a toast.

'Here's to us — the Sassy Sisters, our amazingly gorgeous tower room and our newest member, Smudge!'

Meow, said Smudge.

'The Sassy Sisters,' we all cried, as we laughed and clinked our jars together.

BELLA'S MANGO MADNESS SMOOTHIE RECIPE

Serves 4

2 RIPE MANGOES (FRESH OR FROZEN)

1 FROZEN BANANA

½ PINEAPPLE, CHOPPED

1 DOLLOP OF GREEK YOGHURT

1 CUP OF MILK

½ CUP OF ICE

1 TEASPOON OF HONEY, IF EXTRA SWEETNESS NEEDED

MINT LEAVES (OPTIONAL)

1. ADD INGREDIENTS TO BLENDER.
2. BLEND UNTIL SMOOTH AND FROTHY.
3. SERVE IN JAM JARS WITH FRUIT GARNISH.
4. ENJOY!

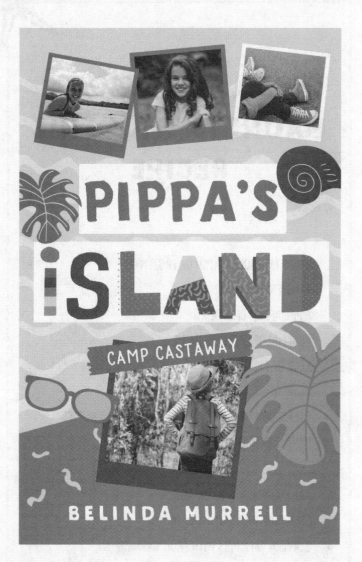

PIPPA'S iSLAND

CAMP CASTAWAY

BELINDA MURRELL

CAMP CASTAWAY

The students in class 5M are heading off to school camp. Pippa has never been away on camp before, at least not to a deserted tropical island! The Sassy Sisters are looking forward to five blissful days together exploring Shipwreck Island's beaches and lagoon. But when the teams get regrouped, Pippa has to learn to cooperate with Olivia and the other girls.

Mrs Marshall promised challenges and adventure, but she forgot to mention the pranks. After one too many of the boys' tricks, the girls decide to take their revenge.

Will class 5M survive Camp Castaway?

AVAILABLE APRIL 2018

Read on for a sneak peek!

CHAPTER 1

FAREWELL

It was eight o'clock on a sunny Monday morning and we were waiting for a sailing boat to take us off on an amazing adventure. Meg, Charlie, Cici and I huddled together on the esplanade, jiggling up and down with excitement. Other kids from year five were gathered around in groups, giggling and chatting. Everyone was wearing casual clothes; shorts, T-shirts, caps and runners. Piles of backpacks, sleeping-bags, boxes, surfboards and packages were scattered among the parents and family members waiting to see us off.

The twenty students of 5M at Kira Cove Primary School were heading off for our school camp. The only other time I'd been on a school sleepover back in London, we'd slept overnight in the school hall, eaten pizza and watched movies. Things couldn't be more different here. This time our school camp would be on a deserted island located in the middle of the ocean, more than an hour north of Kira Island by boat. And we would be away from home for five whole days.

'Seb said it's the best fun,' said Charlie, hugging her guitar in her arms. Her stepbrother was in year six, so he'd been on the camp last year. 'There's no one else there.'

'Jack said they saw some incredible wildlife, like turtles and dolphins and stingrays,' added Meg. 'The island is quite small. You can walk all over it. And you do lots of really fun activities – like snorkelling, bushwalking and playing games.'

'It sounds brilliant,' I said, but I felt a familiar fluttering in my tummy. I was a teensy bit nervous about going away on my first real school camp. I'd never been away from my family for more than a night at a time.

A large white catamaran skimmed towards the wharf, its sails billowing in the breeze. Two crew members in navy shirts ran back and forth on the deck, hauling ropes and pulling down sails. The captain was at the helm, turning the chrome steering wheel and calling orders. One of the crew jumped onto the wharf and tied a thick rope to the pylon. We all surged towards the jetty leading out over the water.

Mrs Marshall stood in front of us with a clipboard. 'Good morning, 5M,' she said with a warm smile. 'Our trusty sailing vessel, the *Wandering Albatross*, has arrived. So it's time to say goodbye to your families, gather your belong-ings and go aboard.'

There was a loud babble of noise as everyone rushed to say goodbye to their parents. I saw Olivia hugging her mum, who was wearing a smart trouser suit and high heels. A younger boy stood by, with similar dark hair and blue eyes, who must be her brother.

Our four families were standing together chatting. Mum was holding our puppy, Summer, by her red lead. Summer jumped up and down with delight to see me. It was as though I'd been gone for days rather than just a few minutes. I wondered how she'd react when I came home on Friday afternoon after nearly a week away.

I said goodbye to Harry and Bella.

Bella was wearing her fluffy green dinosaur tail over her denim shorts. She squeezed me hard around my waist as though she didn't want to let go.

'Don't go away, Pippa,' said Bella, her voice muffled. 'I want you to stay here with us.'

I hugged her back then gently peeled her arms away.

'I'll be back soon, Bella-boo,' I said. 'Look after Summer and Smudge for me.'

I crouched down and took our puppy in my arms, stroking her velvety ears. 'Be a good girl while I'm away, Summer,' I whispered. 'I'll miss you.' Summer licked me gently as though to say 'I'll miss you too'.

Then Mum hugged me long and tight. 'Have the most wonderful time, my darling Pipkin,' she said. 'I love you to the moon and back again.'

'Love you too, Mum,' I said.

'Goodbye, Pipkin,' she said, kissing me on top of my wild, curly hair.

'Bye, Mum,' I replied, giving her a last-minute squeeze. I felt a prickle of tears. Harry was already kicking a ball around with some other kids, while Bella had dashed off to play a chasing game with Charlie's little sister Daisy.

Mum stroked my cheek and gave me a mischievous smile. 'You'll have the most amazing fun – and there might be a little surprise on board.'

'What surprise?' I asked, immediately superduper curious. 'What do you mean?'

'I'm not telling,' said Mum, shaking her head. 'You'll have to wait and see.'

The other girls had already said goodbye to their families and were waiting for me over by the wharf. Meg was carrying her surfboard.

'Pippa, come *on*,' called Charlie. 'If you don't hurry, we'll sail off without you.'

I hoisted up my heavy backpack and trudged over to join the girls. Lots of people were already on board while others queued across the gangplank, carrying their bags and chattering madly. Rory and Sam were just in front of us with Alex, nursing a set of homemade bongo drums. Alex grinned at me and rapped out a rhythmic drum beat with his knuckles.

Towards the front of the cabin there was a familiar-looking girl with red hair tied back in a ponytail. She was directing the kids to stow their luggage in a huge mound in the corner.

'Zoe!' I cried, dropping my backpack on the floor. 'What are you doing here?'

The girls and I crowded around her, calling out greetings. Zoe grinned at us, her silver hoop earrings swinging. 'Hello, girls. I'm your new camp supervisor.'

'What do you mean?' I asked. 'What about the cafe?'

'Last night I had a phone call from Nigel asking me if I could fill in for my friend Lisa, who's come down with a nasty stomach bug,' explained Zoe. 'Nigel and Lisa usually help run the camp.'

Zoe waved her hand towards an older man who was hoisting the heavy eskies into a neat block. It was Nigel, the Kira Beach surf life-saving patrol captain and a regular customer at the cafe. He waved back at us.

'I rang your mum to ask if it was okay for me to have the week off and she said yes straight away. She was so excited I'd be helping out on your school camp,' continued Zoe. 'Nigel is running the water safety program for the camp and I'll be running the land-based activities.'

I looked around at the other girls with delight. We all loved Zoe, the bubbly, eighteen-year-old barista at the Beach Shack Cafe who looked after us so well.

'*You* must be the surprise that Mum was telling me about,' I said. 'It's a shame Lisa is sick but I'm so glad you'll be with us on camp.'

'That's so cool,' said Charlie, lying her guitar down on a seat.

'And that means we can chill out and relax,' said Cici. 'My brother says the camp super-visors can be really tough.'

Zoe's green eyes twinkled with humour. 'Oh no you won't, Cecilia Mee-Shen Lin. I'll be the toughest camp supervisor *ever.*'

We all giggled with disbelief. Zoe was kind, caring and warm-hearted. None of us could ever imagine her being strict with us.

'Okay. Everyone up on deck,' instructed Mrs Marshall. 'It's time to cast off.'

We all scurried up the stairs and onto the deck. Mrs Marshall introduced us to Captain Bellamy and the *Wandering Albatross* crew, George and Hannah. Captain Bellamy stood with her legs apart, one hand on her hip as she directed us where to sit. We perched on the cabin roof. Our parents and families crowded on the wharf, waving and calling farewell. All twenty of us waved and shouted back.

'Bye, Mum. Bye, Summer. Bye, Harry and Bella.' I waved until my arm ached.

The crew cast off the mooring lines and then we were away, the engine chugging as we zigzagged slowly between the moored yachts and brightly painted fishing boats.

I stared back at my family growing smaller and smaller in the distance, wondering about our journey. What would Camp Castaway be like? What amazing adventures would we have over the next few days?

ABOUT THE AUTHOR

At about the age of eight, Belinda Murrell began writing stirring tales of adventure, mystery and magic in hand-illustrated exercise books. As an adult, she combined two of her great loves – writing and travelling the world – and worked as a travel journalist, technical writer and public relations consultant. Now, inspired by her own three children, Belinda is a bestselling, internationally published children's author. Her previous titles include four picture books, her fantasy adventure series, The Sun

Sword Trilogy, and her seven time-slip adventures, *The Locket of Dreams*, *The Ruby Talisman*, *The Ivory Rose*, *The Forgotten Pearl*, *The River Charm*, *The Sequin Star* and *The Lost Sapphire*.

For younger readers (aged 6 to 9), Belinda has the Lulu Bell series about friends, family, animals and adventures growing up in a vet hospital.

Belinda lives in Manly in a gorgeous old house overlooking the sea with her husband, Rob, her three beautiful children, Sammy the Stimson's python and her dog, Rosie. She is an Author Ambassador for Room to Read and Books in Homes.

Find out more about Belinda at her website: **www.belindamurrell.com.au**

Adventures are more fun with friends!
There are thirteen gorgeous Lulu Bell
stories for you to discover.

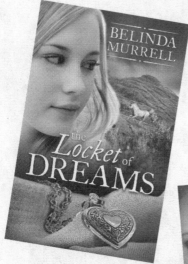

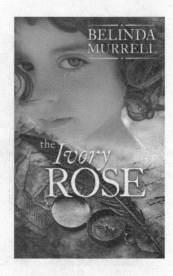

Love history? Escape to another time
with Belinda's seven beautiful
time-slip adventures.

If you love fantasy stories, you'll love
Belinda's Sun Sword trilogy.